RANDOM KILLER

If you were psychotic and you wanted to kill famous people at random, you couldn't find a better hunting ground than the Hotel Beaumont. It is the top luxury hotel anywhere and it will cost you an arm and a leg to stay there overnight and enjoy its fabulous service, its gourmet foods, its incomparable wines, its quiet elegance.

But you do not expect murder as part of the service . . .

RANDOM KILLER

Hugh Pentecost

KEYHOLE CRIME
London · Sydney

First published in Great Britain 1980 by
Robert Hale Limited

Copyright © 1979 Judson Philips

Australian copyright 1981

Philippine copyright 1981

This edition published 1981 by
Keyhole Crime, 15-16 Brook's Mews,
London W1A 1DR

ISBN 0 263 73528 1

Made and printed in Great Britain by
Cox & Wyman Ltd., Reading

Part One

CHAPTER ONE

I suppose if you were psychotic and you wanted to kill famous people at random, you couldn't find a better hunting ground than the Hotel Beaumont. You have only to knock on the next door to your own to encounter someone who is famous for something, if only the possession of a great deal of money. You don't stay at the Beaumont without at least that one claim to fame. It is the top luxury hotel anywhere and it will cost you an arm and a leg to stay there overnight and enjoy its fabulous service, its gourmet foods, its incomparable wines, its quiet elegance. You can buy a cooperative apartment in the Beaumont if you can get up several hundred thousand dollars, and the annual maintenance will be more than the average man earns in any one year of his life.

Its location on New York's East Side makes it a home-away-from-home for foreign diplomats concerned with the operation of the United Nations. Movie stars on the move, today's young millionaires in the world of sports, corporate executives with six-figure salaries and limitless expense accounts, Arab oil billionaires are all patrons of this legendary hotel. It is like a small city, operating almost isolated from the rest of the world, with its own shops, a bank, restaurants and bars, a hospital, elegant rooms for elegant parties large and small, its own security force. Sitting on top of this extravagant world is a man who built the legend and is an essential part of it. He is Pierre Chambrun, a short, dark, square little man with bright black eyes buried in deep pouches, who can look like a compassionate father confessor or a hanging judge depending on his mood of the moment. The Beaumont is *his* hotel. He owns a piece of it and his board of directors wouldn't dream of interfering with any move he makes. He is the Man who makes the Beaumont what it is. He knows everything that goes on, on every one of its forty floors, every minute of every hour of every day and week, of every month and year. We on his staff claim that he has a special built-in radar system. The truth is that no one who works for him, from the lowest busboy to his incredible secretary Miss Betsy Ruysdale, would think of not reporting the slightest thing out of order directly to him. He knows how to handle any emergency and he will take the responsibility for that handling. If any of his people try to deal with a problem without reporting to him, and something goes wrong, then that person will be out on the street on his or her rump.

But Chambrun cannot always foresee trouble that comes from the outside. The little city that is the Beaumont is contaminated on occasion by violence, which is part of today's world. It's like a plague that strikes before you can be aware that it's within the walls.

So it was that murder struck at us on a gentle spring day that year, murder so grim that it threatened to destroy Pierre Chambrun's world.

I am Mark Haskell, in charge of public relations for the Beaumont. I have just celebrated my tenth anniversary in the job, and, without self-flattery, I think I can say that I

4

know more about the intimate workings of the hotel than anyone with the exceptions of the Man himself, Betsy Ruysdale, his personal secretary, and Jerry Dodd, our chief of security. In the old days Jerry would have been called the house dick. The four of us constitute a sort of upper-echelon brain trust. In theory we know everything there is to know, and pass on to people in the lower brackets only what is important to their functioning. I say "in theory" because on that spring morning none of us knew that there was a killer loose somewhere in the sacred confines of the Beaumont who was about to turn the smooth working of a sort of Swiss watch machine into something approximating a madhouse.

There is a paradox involving the handling of the famous people who are guests of the Beaumont. Some of them come there because it is *the* place to be seen. It is my job to let the media know that a glamorous movie star, a political hotshot, a notable writer, or a ballet artist is a guest. Instantly the reporters, photographers, interviewers, and the general public swarm over us to get a look at the "stars." But the same kinds of people may inform us that they want to be anonymous, unnoticed, their presence in the hotel, perhaps in the city itself, kept secret. We can handle that just as efficiently as we can provide notoriety. The current Clark Gable, whoever he may be, can stay at the Beaumont, his presence undetected, his comings and goings carefully shielded. He is given what is called "the John Smith treatment," and not a maid, a waiter, a bellboy, or a desk clerk will whisper the fact of his presence to anyone.

That particular spring day when all hell broke loose in the hotel began as every day begins for me on the job. I am called by the switchboard at nine o'clock. Since my nighttime duties keep me on the go till all hours of the morning, that isn't what could be called sleeping late. My apartment—a sitting room, bedroom, bath, and kitchenette—is on the second floor of the hotel, just down the hall from Chambrun's office. My own office is on the same floor. I plug in the coffee percolator, shave, shower, and dress. I have a glass of juice, an English muffin, sometimes with jam, and coffee. At precisely nine forty-five I present myself to Chambrun in his office.

Chambrun may have been up much later than I, but he arrives in his office from his penthouse on the roof at exactly nine o'clock. Waiting for him, every day, is Miss Ruysdale, looking fresh and lovely whatever her nightlife may have been, and Monsieur Fresney, the number one chef at the breakfast hour. On a sideboard are selections of food, ranging from bacon or ham to a small filet mignon, to a broiled salmon steak with béarnaise sauce, to Chambrun's favorite, old-fashioned chicken hash. There are eggs to be prepared in a chafing dish in any fashion the Man suggests. There is a choice of gluten bread or English muffins, which he eats with sweet butter and wild strawberry jam imported from Devonshire in England. There is American coffee, to be distinguished from the Turkish coffee he drinks all day, prepared for him in a samovar on the sideboard by Miss Ruysdale. No juice or fruit. He takes those on the run during the day. He will not eat again until a gourmet dinner at nine in the evening.

Each morning Chambrun makes his choice, eats with relish, lights one of his flat Egyptian cigarettes with his second cup of coffee, and glances at the door. I am supposed to be there, coming in from Miss Ruysdale's outer office. He doesn't have to look at his watch to know that it is precisely nine forty-five and that only an earthquake could prevent my appearing on the dot.

Miss Ruysdale—he calls her "Ruysdale" in a sort of neutering process although most of us are convinced she is something more to him than an indispensable management aide—follows me in, carrying a stack of cards, which represent the new guests who have checked in since the morning before.

6

Hotel guests might have been a little uneasy if they had seen those cards. Each one is an intimate and very personal dossier. Symbols indicate credit ratings; personal habits such as alcoholism or woman chasing (man chasing if it is a woman); business, professional, and social friends; past performances as guests of the Beaumont. If Chambrun's initials are on the card, it means he has special information about that specific guest.

Chambrun's office is not like an office at all, really. It is like a very elegant living room except for the carved Florentine desk behind which he sits after breakfast, fingering the cards Ruysdale has brought him. The Turkish rug, the drapes, the antiques, the blue-period Picasso, a gift from the artist, which peers down at him from the opposite wall, are not what you expect to find in a business office. There are no filing cabinets or safes. On the desk are a telephone and what I call a squawk box, to which he can transfer a phone call and make it audible to anyone else who may be in the room with him.

On that fateful spring morning Chambrun was looking at the registration cards and Ruysdale and I were waiting for some comment from him when the little red light blinked on his phone. There is no bell or buzzer.

Ruysdale picked up the receiver and answered. "It's Mrs. Kniffin, the head housekeeper," Ruysdale said.

Chambrun leaned forward and turned on the squawk box. "I know who Mrs. Kniffin is," he said dryly. Then, to the caller, "Yes, Mrs. Kniffin?"

"There is a dead man in thirty-four-oh-six," Mrs. Kniffin said in a shaken voice.

"Name?" Chambrun said, his own voice gone flat.

"Mr. Geoffrey Hammond," the housekeeper said.

"Oh, brother!" I heard myself say.

I don't think there are many readers who won't know who Geoffrey Hammond is—or was. That handsome dark face, that clipped British voice, had invaded millions of homes in America over the years. He was as familiar to television viewers as Walter Cronkite, or as Edward R. Murrow in another generation, or perhaps David Frost would come closer today. He had started out twenty years ago as a news analyst for the BBC in London. It had fallen to him to interview some of the political hotshots in the Middle East and Israel during the fifties and sixties. American television had lured him away from his homeland with a huge financial bait, and he had become the man who interviewed all the important people in the world for International. Controversial, but with an audience so large that sponsoring advertisers battled to the death trying to buy time on his shows. Something like a gold mine had passed on into the next world if Mrs. Kniffin was right.

I had a small hope that Mrs. Kniffin was wrong, as Chambrun and I headed for the thirty-fourth floor. Ruysdale stayed behind to alert security and hold the fort there. Understand, I had no doubt that there was a dead man in 3406. The small hope I mentioned was not that death would go away from us, but that the dead man might not be Geoffrey Hammond. Let it be a friend of Hammond's, his male secretary, anyone but Hammond. That wasn't because I had any affection or personal regard for Hammond. In my book he was an arrogant sonofabitch. But a dead Geoffrey Hammond would bring the news media from all around the world cascading down on us; the smooth routines of the hotel would be disrupted. On the way up to thirty-four in the elevator with Chambrun I was ticking off on my fingers the number of events scheduled for that day in the hotel. There were to be five special dinners held in five of our very special private dining rooms; a big blowout by the Parker Foundation to be held in the grand ballroom; an all-day session in the executive suite for the top brass of a big multinational corporation, oil the main topic of discussion. And it went on and on, from a fashion show to a photography exhibit.

Shout the news of Geoffrey Hammond's death and every one of these events would be in some way dislocated.

And Geoffrey Hammond was dead. Worse than just being dead from natural causes, he had been violently executed.

Jerry Dodd had beaten us to thirty-four. He is a wiry, dark, intense little man who always seems to be angry. He had been an FBI agent before Chambrun recruited him to the top security job in the Beaumont. He knows his job and is better at it than most people ever get to be.

Jerry opened the door of 3406 to us, and the look he gave Chambrun told us all we needed to know. The news was bad.

"Not pretty," Jerry said.

"Hammond?" Chambrun asked.

"In what you might say was the flesh," Jerry said. "And it wasn't a heart attack, Mr. Chambrun."

"What, then?"

"Better see for yourself," Jerry said.

No two suites in the Beaumont are decorated and furnished alike. It was no accident that 3406 had been assigned to Hammond. There were British hunting prints on the walls, panels consisting of brilliantly painted coats of arms of famous British families. The furniture was heavy and solid enough to have accommodated knights in armor.

My first look at the way it now was didn't instantly suggest violence. Except that one heavy armchair had fallen over backwards and that behind it, covered by a sheet, must be the body of a dead man, the place looked in order.

"Room-service waiter came for the breakfast wagon and found him," Jerry said.

The wagon was there. It had been set up in front of the tipped-over armchair. A straight-backed chair had faced the armchair.

"He had company," Chambrun said.

Jerry nodded. "Service for two. Juice, eggs and bacon, toast and coffee. Two of everything."

"How?" Chambrun asked.

"Brace yourself," Jerry said.

He bent down and pulled back the sheet. I remember turning away, wondering where the bathroom was. I thought I was going to be sick.

Hammond, in life, had been an almost too handsome man, elegant bone structure; bright, inquisitive, sardonic blue eyes; a strong, straight mouth. What was there now was a horror. Wide-open eyes bulged out of his head. His mouth was grotesquely twisted open and swollen, his black tongue protruded from it. It was like a ghastly mask out of a horror movie.

"Garroted," I heard Jerry say. "Picture wire. Done from behind the poor bastard."

"No real struggle," Chambrun said.

"No. Someone he didn't suspect came up behind him. He never got out of the chair. In tightening the wire the killer finally pulled it over backwards—toward him."

"Did the room-service waiter see who the breakfast guest was?" Chambrun asked.

"No. He brought the wagon, Hammond told him to just leave it there in front of the armchair. No one in sight."

"Man or woman?"

"Hell, boss, I only got here about three minutes before you did," Jerry said.

"Looked in the bedroom?"

"Only to make sure there was nobody there."

"You called Homicide?"

"We got lucky," Jerry said. "Lieutenant Hardy's on his way."

Hardy is an old friend who has handled other violences at the Beaumont.

Chambrun looked at me. I had seen the cold fury in his eyes before, the thin, straight set to his mouth. Jerry Dodd had commented on that look once, long ago. "Someone

10

just fouled his nest." They say a drowning man sees his whole life parade before him just before he goes down for the third time. Chambrun, I knew, was seeing projections of the future. He was seeing what would happen to our carefully disciplined existence when the word got out that Geoffrey Hammond had been murdered in the Beaumont.

"How long have we got, Mark?" he asked me.

He meant how long did we have until the news broke.

"Depends on how urgently somebody tries to reach him," I said.

"Alert the switchboard. Get them to take messages. Anything to stall."

"If Hardy comes steaming up here in a police car with the sirens going, we've had it," Jerry Dodd said.

"Hardy won't do that," Chambrun said. He knew his man.

CHAPTER TWO

The next hour comes back to me, as I write this, in disconnected fragments. I was reminded of something I should have remembered by Mrs. Veach, the chief day-time operator on the hotel switchboard. Geoffrey Hammond, on this particular visit to the Beaumont, was a "John Smith." His presence was to be kept secret. He was registered under another name. As far as anyone knew, who didn't know Hammond by sight, the occupant of Room 3406 was one Roy Conklin. "Roy Conklin" wasn't a phony name, however. There was a real Roy Conklin and he was Hammond's business manager, agent, publicity genius. I knew Conklin by sight from other Hammond visits to the Beaumont, a prematurely grey, bitter-faced

11

man, who walked with a severe limp, the result of war wounds I'd been told. I don't think I knew what war.

"Conklin" had been registered in 3406 for four days, and Mrs. Veach couldn't recall any in-coming phone calls. Certainly there had been no calls for Geoffrey Hammond, who wasn't supposed to be there.

None of this, you understand, was particularly unusual. The fact that Hammond was registered under his manager's name was noted on the registration card. It was not a secret kept from the front desk or from Chambrun, for that matter, who had seen the card the morning after Hammond was registered. We had covered up for famous people like this time and time again.

Roy Conklin was going to have to be found and notified that his distinguished client was dead. That could wait, however, until Lieutenant Hardy was in charge, which would be very shortly.

Jerry Dodd's office would have notified the various command posts that we had a disaster. My job was to fend off the outside world for the moment. The minute I hit the lobby I sensed that Mr. Atterbury on the front desk, Johnny Thacker, the day bell captain, and his crew were aware of what was up. No one asked me what was new, but the question was on half a dozen faces.

I was looking for the unwanted sign that the press was in attendance. It was only a little after ten, which is normally early for news people who are just looking for scraps of gossip. They usually don't appear until the lunch hour when the famous and notorious gather for the first martini of the day. Today, worse luck, was different. The oil company executives were meeting in the Palm Room, and where there is oil in this day and age there is news. Half a dozen reporters who weren't gossip collectors were watching the corridor that led to the Palm Room, among them Dick Barrows of the *Times*, who is a very shrewd operator indeed. He spotted me as I stood there wonder-

12

ing how to keep them occupied when Hardy arrived. All they had to do was get a glimpse of the Homicide man and we had trouble.

"Hi, Mark," Dick Barrows said. "What's new?"

"It's the third of May nineteen seventy-eight," I said. "It's the first time it's ever been that."

"Ho, ho, ho!" Dick said. He is a pleasant-faced, sandy-haired guy with very direct grey eyes. "Kid me not, friend. I have an instinct for the offbeat."

"Oil prices are going up—or down," I said.

"Screw oil prices," Dick said. "I see one of your security people report something to Atterbury on the front desk, and Mr. A promptly goes into shock. I see the same security man report to your bell captain, who passes it on to his boys, who all suddenly take on the look of CIA agents who have blown their cover."

"Tip on the feature race at Belmont," I said. "They're all anticipating making a fortune on a long shot. The security man is the hotel bookmaker."

Dick was looking past me across the lobby. "And I now see a well-known homicide detective wandering toward the elevators as though he was looking for the men's room. What room is he really looking for, Mark?"

"Keep those other guys distracted and I'll give you the inside track," I told him.

He was watching Hardy disappear into an elevator. "I trust you with my life but not with my career," he said. He was watching the floor indicator move upward outside the shaft of the elevator Hardy had taken. It would stop at thirty-four and that would be that. "Who collected what, Mark?"

"We need a little time for Hardy to get plugged in," I said.

"Who?" Dick said, still watching the indicator.

I had to play ball with him or have the whole army down on us. "Special to the *Times*," I said, "in return for keeping it strictly to yourself."

13

The elevator indicator had stopped at thirty-four. Dick gave me a twisted little smile. "Scout's honor," he said.

"Geoffrey Hammond," I said.

Dick shook his head. "I share nothing with that bastard," he said.

"You're not listening," I said. "Hardy is here to investigate Geoffrey Hammond's murder."

Dick looked at me, his eyes widening. "You're kidding!"

"I wish I was," I said. "Thirty-four-oh-six in fifteen minutes—if you keep the others off us."

Dick grinned. "Chambrun must be boiling," he said. "No one that important has a right to get killed in his hotel."

Our Richard wasn't far off the mark. But, I noticed, not shocked by the news. I was to realize before too much time had passed that Geoffrey Hammond was not loved by many people.

A note about Betsy Ruysdale, who was my next port of call. She looks taller than she is because she carries herself so well, straight and lithe. I'm guessing that she is in her late thirties, but she could be more or less. Someone has said that the older a woman gets the better she gets—up to a point, I suppose. Betsy Ruysdale is well within that point, whatever it is. She is handsome, well groomed, her hair a reddish blond. She dresses conservatively in the office. Chambrun wouldn't want messenger boys hanging around making eyes at some chick. I've seen her at a couple of swank evening functions in the hotel, dressed to kill, and she is gorgeous. I might have had dreams about her if I hadn't been convinced that Chambrun was both her business and her private life.

As a secretary she is fantastic. As far as Chambrun is concerned she reads his mind. He orders something done and it has been done before he mentions it. He wants something from the office files and Ruysdale already has it in her hands. She and Chambrun are tuned in on exactly the same wavelength. About a year ago Chambrun disap-

14

peared, without explanation, from the hotel for twenty-four hours. The person who took charge in his absence was Betsy Ruysdale. No one debated it. Every detail that Chambrun had at his fingertips was also at hers.

Betsy Ruysdale is a very special person and, secretly, I am quite mad for her. But that morning was not a time for daydreams.

One of the girls from the stenographic pool was at Ruysdale's desk in the outer office when I got there. Ruysdale was in Chambrun's office, at the command post. Evidently orders were coming down from 3406.

"We'd better try to locate Roy Conklin," I said.

"He's on his way," Ruysdale said.

I should have known. I told her that I'd had to spill the beans to Dick Barrows in order to keep the other reporters out of our hair. She nodded approval, I thought.

"Hammond evidently wasn't popular with his peers," I said.

"To put it mildly," Ruysdale said.

"It would seem he was having breakfast with someone who didn't like him," I said.

She gave me a thoughtful look. "Jerry doesn't think we can assume that," she said. "The person who had breakfast with him could have left before the killer appeared on the scene. Odd thing, Mark. Hammond was a very busy man, on the go every second—appointments, interviews—but Jerry hasn't found any kind of appointment book, any addresses or telephone numbers. First thing he looked for, to see who was due for breakfast."

"Maybe Conklin handles all that for him."

Ruysdale tapped a green leather notebook on Chambrun's desk. "Pierre keeps more in his head than any man I ever knew," she said. "But appointments and special phone numbers are written down for him. I do it for him if he neglects to. Conklin isn't around to do my kind of job."

"Jerry thinks somebody stole an appointment book?"

"I'd steal it, wouldn't you, if you didn't want anyone to know you'd had breakfast with him?"

"Sounds logical," I said.

"No other signs of robbery," Ruysdale said. "Money, watch, jewelry like pearl dress studs, all untouched. But no record of any appointments."

"He must have had appointments lined up for the day," I said. "He wouldn't be sitting around playing solitaire in his room, even if he was keeping his presence here a secret. Where did you find Conklin?"

"At his office, just a few blocks down Madison Avenue. He should be here any moment."

"I'd better get upstairs before Dick Barrows starts hammering on the door of thirty-four-oh-six," I said.

Ruysdale opened a drawer of the desk and produced a flat box of Egyptian cigarettes. "Better take these to Pierre," she said. "In his present state of mind he should be just about out of them by now."

She knew his needs before he was aware of them himself.

Lieutenant Hardy, a big, blond, rather clumsy-looking man, appears more like a slightly bewildered professional fullback than a very shrewd expert in the field of crime. Whatever he looks like, he is one of the very best at his job. He and Chambrun work well together because their approaches are so different. Chambrun is a hunch player whose hunches are almost always solid. He is mercurial, arriving at answers without bothering to gather facts that will prove out his instinctive processes. Hardy is an evidence gatherer, slow, plodding, but never leaving a single stone unturned until he has covered every inch of the territory. He knows he has to build a case for a district attorney. Chambrun only wants an answer for himself. Combining their talents they are a very tough team.

One of Jerry Dodd's security boys was on guard outside 3406, but I was ushered in without question. The living room was crowded. Evidently Hardy's homicide crew, fingerprint boys, and police photographers, had come up by a service elevator and were hard at work. A young Chinese doctor from the medical examiner's office was kneeling beside what was left of Geoffrey Hammond. Hardy didn't waste time.

The blond detective, Chambrun, and Jerry Dodd were in a huddle at the far end of the room. I joined them, weaving my way through the army of technicians. Hardy gave me a cheerful nod.

"How come you cruised through the lobby instead of coming up the back way with your boys?" I asked him. "Dick Barrows of the *Times* spotted you and I had to fill him in to keep a whole army off our backs."

"I wanted to be seen," Hardy said.

"By whom?"

"I wish I knew," Hardy said.

I had to let that one lie where it was because Chambrun, cold as ice, was at me.

"Roy Conklin is on his way," he said. "Hardy doesn't want him up here. He's to be taken to my office. Hold his hand until Hardy and I can get there. You might ask him about women."

"What women?"

"A woman spent a good part of the night here—may have breakfasted with Hammond."

"How do you know?"

Jerry Dodd grinned at me. "Go smell the bedsheets and the pillowcase," he said. "Unless Hammond wears Chanel Number Five, he had company."

"Now!" Chambrun said to me.

Mine not to reason why. I made tracks for the second floor and Chambrun's office.

Roy Conklin was already there, storming up and down Chambrun's office on his gimpy leg, shouting at Betsy Ruysdale and two security boys who were preventing him from taking off. I have described him as prematurely grey, bitter faced. He was in a rage now.

"You can't keep me here," he was telling the world. "It's false arrest. I'll have you all and this hotel sued out of your socks before I'm done with you."

"Mr. Chambrun and Lieutenant Hardy will be here in a few minutes," I told him. "I'm Mark Haskell, public relations for the hotel. Hammond's room is full of technicians at the moment. No place to talk."

"I don't want to talk! I want to see for myself!"

"You wouldn't like it," I said.

"Maybe you'd be good enough to tell me just what has happened," Conklin said. "Nobody else has bothered."

I told him. Hammond strangled with picture wire from behind. An unknown breakfast guest. An unknown woman in his bed. As I talked, Conklin lowered himself into one of the office's leather armchairs, as though his leg and a half wouldn't hold him up any longer.

"Where is Bobby?" he asked.

"Bobby who?"

"Geoff's secretary."

"Does she wear Chanel Number Five?" I asked.

"Bobby is a 'he,' for Christ sake," Conklin said. "Bobby Bryan. He's undoubtedly the one who had breakfast with Geoff. He usually had breakfast with him to set up the day."

"This Bryan scheduled the appointments? The cops wondered about not finding any appointment book, with addresses, telephone numbers, and like that."

"Geoff didn't have one. Couldn't be bothered. Bobby handles all that. He probably had breakfast and took off on errands."

"After strangling Hammond?" I suggested.

"You goddamned imbecile!" Conklin shouted at me. "Bobby is Geoff's closest and most trusted friend."

"Can you suggest who the woman might be who spent the night with Hammond?" I asked.

Conklin gave me a twisted, sardonic smile. "I doubt if

18

any woman spent the night with him. Oh, I'm not saying there wasn't a woman. I'm saying that she did what she was paid to do and took off, long before breakfast. He couldn't bear to have women around after—after the fact."

"Paid?" I said. "You mean he was partial to call girls?"

"Romance wasn't Geoff's dish," Conklin said. "He got what he wanted, paid the bill, and had no obligations. Place like this is always loaded with fancy tarts. Why don't you ask the head of the union?"

I hate to admit he was right. High-class call girls are always available in the best hotels. It goes with the territory. We police the situation pretty well but it exists.

"Bobby can probably tell you when he turns up," Conklin said. "He not only arranges Geoff's business appointments but also his pleasures."

So where the hell was Mr. Bobby Bryan?

"We thought you were the one who handled Hammond's affairs," I said. "Business manager, agent, public relations?"

"I am all those things," Conklin said, "which doesn't include picking up women for him, or buying his razor blades, or keeping track of his nonbusiness dates."

"He's registered here in your name," I said.

"With the full knowledge of Mr. Chambrun and your reservations department. There were business reasons for his wanting to stay obscure on this visit."

"Are those reasons a secret?"

He pushed himself up out of his chair and limped toward me. I swear I thought he was going to take a swing at me. "What are you, Haskell, the cops or something? You can take your questions and stuff them!"

"He's not the cops," Chambrun said from behind me. He and Hardy were in the doorway. "But he asks perfectly reasonable and intelligent questions."

Chambrun walked over to his desk and sat down. Miss

19

Ruysdale pushed a memo pad in front of him on which she'd made notes.

"Hammond's secretary, one Robert Bryan, has a single room on the fourth floor," Chambrun said. "He doesn't answer his phone."

Ruysdale had been at work while I was talking to Conklin. She never misses.

"So he's out somewhere," Conklin said. "Is he supposed to check with you on where he's going or what he does?"

"No," Chambrun said. He looked a question at me.

I brought him up to date on Bryan, his habit of breakfasting with Hammond, and his special job, which indicated that the lady who had been in Hammond's bed wasn't a lady.

"So we come back to Mark's last question," Chambrun said. He fished in his pocket for a cigarette, came up empty, and I handed him the box Ruysdale had given me. She brought him a demitasse of Turkish coffee from the sideboard. He had everything he needed except answers.

"What questions?" Conklin asked.

"Why was he registered in your name?" Hardy asked, speaking for the first time.

"He had the right to stay under cover if he wanted to, didn't he?" Conklin was still burning.

"We can go on with this at police headquarters if you like, Mr. Conklin," Hardy said.

"Don't try to strong-arm me, Lieutenant!" Conklin said.

"I can be patient for about two minutes," Hardy said.

Conklin seemed to make the intelligent assessment that he was up against someone he couldn't bluff or browbeat. He retreated to his chair and sat down again. He raised his hands and pressed their palms against his eyes for a second.

"This is a deep personal loss and a severe business crisis for me," he said, lowering his hands. "I'm afraid I'm not thinking very clearly."

"Take your time," Hardy said. He glanced at Ruysdale.

"Perhaps Mr. Conklin won't mind if you turn on the tape recorder, Miss Ruysdale." Conklin looked up, his eyes narrowed. "Just so we don't have to go over and over it, Mr. Conklin. If you don't like it when it's done, we'll throw it out."

The tape recorder is kept in Chambrun's desk drawer. Ruysdale turned it on. Believe it or not, I don't know where the microphones are hidden in that office.

"The question is," Hardy said, "why was Hammond staying under cover, registered in your name, Mr. Conklin?"

Conklin drew a deep breath. This was for the record. You could sense his need for care and caution. "The poor sonofabitch was famous," he said. "You know that. Most of the time he enjoyed what that brought him, big shots fawning over him, women being quite open in their admiration, even autograph collectors. He liked being famous. But there were times in his business, in his profession, when privacy was important."

"His business, I understand, is interviewing important people for television," Hardy said.

Conklin hesitated. "That's his business, his profession."

"But he uses his contacts for personal advantages?" Chambrun asked, his eyes narrowed against the smoke from his cigarette.

"Doesn't everyone?" Conklin said, his voice harsh.

"We're still at square one, Mr. Conklin," Hardy said. "Why what Chambrun calls 'the John Smith treatment' this time?"

"He is—or was—about to tape an interview," Conklin said. "Tomorrow—it was to have been. It was to be with one of the leaders of the Palestine Liberation group. It's not a popular project in a Jew-ridden city like this. If some Zionist hoodlums got wind of it, Geoff might have been in physical danger."

Chambrun was suddenly sitting up very straight in his chair. He didn't like what he'd heard."

"You are anti-Semitic, Mr. Conklin?" he asked, his voice cold.

Conklin gave him a level stare. "How I feel isn't important," he said.

"It's important to me," Chambrun said. "I won't listen to that kind of garbage in this office."

Hardy ignored the exchange. "It seems he was in physical danger," he said. "In spades."

"It's a controversial subject," Conklin said. "That stupid, gun-toting Arafat appears before the United Nations and creates a crazy image of the Palestinian people. They have a case, you know. Geoff was going to see to it that their story was properly told. There are certainly people who don't want that to happen." He glanced at Chambrun. "Prejudiced people."

"So help me—" Chambrun began.

"Where was this interview, this taping, to take place?" Hardy interrupted smoothly.

"A sound studio has been rented, over on Broadway," Conklin said. "Our own technicians would have handled it. It's been in the planning for about three months. I could have sworn not a word about it had leaked out. Silence was as important to Zadir as it was to us."

"Zadir?" Hardy asked.

It was Chambrun who answered. "Rhaman Zadir, a Palestinian soldier of fortune. An artist at terrorism."

Conklin shrugged, as if to say there was no use fighting Chambrun's prejudice.

"If this Zadir was going to have his story told his way, he had no reason to want Hammond hurt," Hardy said.

"Of course not," Conklin said. "But some hot-headed Zionist—"

"Oh, for God's sake!" Chambrun said. "He invites someone who has it in for him for breakfast? Lets an enemy wander around behind him with a garroting wire?"

"I still say it was Bobby Bryan who had breakfast with

him, as he often did," Conklin said. "You'll see when he turns up."

"No one broke into thirty-four-oh-six," Chambrun said. "Hammond let whoever it was in—if there was someone. The person who killed him either had breakfast with him or came in after Bryan left, if you're right about that. Whoever that person was didn't bother Hammond, didn't alarm him. He wasn't prepared for what happened."

"What about Bryan?" Hardy asked. "Were there difficulties between them you haven't mentioned?"

"Bobby is like a son to Geoff," Conklin said.

"Sons have been known to kill their fathers," Hardy said. "I could cite you scores of cases."

"Two people couldn't have been closer," Conklin said.

"What about you, Mr. Conklin?" Chambrun asked. "Where were you for breakfast, or just after breakfast? You handle Hammond's money, his career. Had something gone wrong between you?"

"What bull!" Conklin said.

"You mentioned Zionist hoodlums," Hardy said. "Did you have someone in mind?"

"The woods are full of them," Conklin said. "They're never mentioned in this country's Jewish-controlled press. It's always Arab or Palestinian terrorists who get the headlines."

Chambrun's eyes glittered in narrowed slits. "Suppose you tell us, Mr. Conklin, how you got that bad leg of yours," he said quietly.

I have seen hatred mirrored on human faces in my time, but nothing to equal the murderous look that Conklin gave Chambrun. I think it jarred Hardy, too.

"I don't have time for a private war," he said.

"I have been accused of prejudice," Chambrun said, looking smugly happy. "I think it should be made clear to you, Hardy, that Conklin is at least equally prejudiced. Tell him what happened to your leg, Conklin."

Chambrun evidently knew, but how he had come by

the information I had no idea. Ruysdale, I thought, looked surprised, too. When Conklin didn't respond, Chambrun spelled it out.

"It's no secret," he said, "that Hammond has for a long time been an expert observer of the conflict in the Middle East. It's also no secret that his contacts and his sympathy have been with the Arab cause. There's no law against that. I suspect, however, that Hammond, and probably Conklin, have gotten rich on information and tips passed on by the Arab oil barons. Hammond has covered the action out there for years, has been informed in advance of anti-Israeli moves by Arab terrorists. He has always been on hand to report them, giving the Arab cause a sympathetic coloring. Not popular in this country."

"If you knew or would listen to the facts—" Conklin said.

"A few years back Arab terrorists raided an Israeli settlement in the Sinai," Chambrun said.

"An illegal settlement!" Conklin said.

"Women and children were butchered," Chambrun said. "Hammond and Conklin were there as observers. Hammond would have to justify it later. That's what he got paid for. Israeli commandos appeared out of nowhere and the observers had to take it on the run. Hammond made it, but Mr. Conklin found himself cornered. An Israeli commando didn't have time to take prisoners, but he made sure Conklin would still be around to be picked up later. He fired a round of machine-gun bullets into Conklin's knee and leg. Hammond staged a rescue before a mop-up squad could take Conklin prisoner, but Conklin no longer has a rational view of Jews, or Israelis, or those who sympathize with them."

"Would you, in my place?" Conklin almost shouted. He yanked at his right trouser leg, pulling it up, and revealed a shiny aluminum artificial leg. I noticed his sock was fastened to it with some kind of tape. "Would you love people who left you to hop around the rest of your life on a tin foot?"

Chambrun sipped at his demitasse of Turkish coffee and put the cup down on his desk. "Thirty-odd years ago," he said, "I fought in the French Resistance in Paris. I saw atrocities, cruelties, inflicted by the Nazis on innocent French civilians. I hated the Germans as a people, irrationally and to the death. If, to this day, you hear me take off against a German man, mark it down as not to be trusted. And so, Mr. Conklin, I despise and distrust myself in that area, just as I despise and distrust your remarks about Jews in this city, about the American press, and about 'Zionist hoodlums' who may be responsible for Hammond's murder. You are as sick about Jews as I am about Germans. My point about all this is that Lieutenant Hardy should know that you will even use the death of a friend as a means of striking at a whole nation of people you hate."

The room was deathly still for a moment except for the faint whirring sound of the tape recorder in the desk drawer. The little red light blinked on Chambrun's phone, Miss Ruysdale answered.

"Mr. Robert Bryan is in the outer office," she said.

I got to know and like Bobby Bryan before this grim adventure was finished. He was young, not yet thirty, which is a kid in my book. I am not yet forty. He wears his blond hair crew cut. Short hair is "in" these days. He is so American it's almost funny, and it's surprising that he should have become so close to the British-bred-and-educated Geoffrey Hammond. He wasn't smiling when he came into Chambrun's office that day, but it was almost the only time I was to see him without a smile near the surface, a mischievous humor that was the key to his personality. He was a Brooks Brothers boy, wearing grey flannels and a summer sports jacket, with a pink button-down Brooks shirt and a moderately gay figured blue tie.

25

There was a stunned look in his normally bright blue eyes.

He seemed relieved to see Conklin present. "What in God's name happened, Roy?" he asked.

"Someone strangled him with a wire," Conklin said. Anger had deserted him.

Bobby looked around, bewildered, while Hardy introduced himself and the rest of us.

"Did you have breakfast with Mr. Hammond this morning?" Hardy asked.

"No!"

"Someone did. Do you know who, Mr. Bryan?"

"No!"

"You made his appointments, set up his daily routines for him. And you don't know who was scheduled for breakfast with him this morning?"

"No. I didn't know anyone was supposed to breakfast with him. I—I had some early morning errands to do for him. I just got back to the hotel a few minutes ago. A security man in the lobby told me Geoff was—was dead, and I was to come up here. I just don't believe it! My God, he was so fine, so full of beans the last time I saw him."

"When was that?" Hardy asked.

"Last night about ten o'clock. I went to tell him—" He stopped.

"That you'd arranged for a girl for him?" Hardy asked.

"Oh, brother!" Bobby said.

"It's important we know who that girl was, Mr. Bryan."

"She couldn't have had breakfast with him," Bobby said.

"So who was she?"

For the first time I got a glimpse of Bobby's boyish smile. "You won't believe it, but I don't know," he said.

"You got him a girl and you don't know who she was?"

"That's how it was," Bobby said. Hardy waited for him to go on. "You see, we—Mr. Hammond and I—have stayed at the Beaumont before." He glanced at an impassive Chambrun. "Best hotel—maybe in the whole world,

26

Mr. Chambrun. Mr. Hammond wouldn't dream of staying anywhere else, even when he wanted to stay under cover. 'Most public place in the world where you can be the most private if you ask for it,' Geoff said about the Beaumont."

"The girl, Mr. Bryan," Hardy said sharply.

"So we've stayed here before," Bobby said. "I knew the ropes. You see, when Geoff wants a girl he wants her right then. I have to know, quickly, who to contact, where to go."

"The girl!" Hardy said, out of patience.

"So help me, I'm trying to get to it, Lieutenant," Bobby said. "There is a girl who operates out of the Trapeze Bar, just across the mezzanine from here. Three or four visits ago—through channels, you might say—I unearthed this girl for Geoff. She satisfied. On the next visits I located her again. I was instructed to find her last night."

"Her *name!*" Hardy demanded.

"Dorothy DeLavergne," Bobby said. He laughed outright. "My God, where do they dream up their stage names?"

"Address," Hardy said.

"Slow down, Lieutenant. It wasn't Dorothy who played games with Geoff last night. Incidentally, I don't know her address. I just go looking for her in the Trapeze. I tried to get her address the first time, after Geoff had been pleased with her. She wouldn't give me an address or a phone number. She said I could find her in the Trapeze or, if not, ask Eddie."

"Eddie who?"

"Just Eddie. He's one of the bartenders there."

I confirmed that for Hardy. Chambrun knew how these things worked but I knew he wouldn't want to seem involved. As I've said, the call girls go with the territory.

"Last night Dorothy had what she called 'a previous commitment,' " Bobby said, and laughed again. "But she had a friend she thought would please Geoff. She ought to know what would please him, you see. So I gave her the room number and she said she'd send her friend up. I went upstairs myself to tell Geoff what I'd arranged, and that was the last I saw of him."

"So this girl could have been the one who had breakfast with Hammond," Hardy said.

"I doubt it," Bobby said. "Unless she turned out to be the Queen of Sheba. With Geoff it's 'Take off your clothes, dear'; forty-five athletic minutes in the hay; then 'Put on your clothes, dear.' A hundred and fifty bucks and an extra five for taxi fare. No romantic approach, no chitchat afterwards. It was a standard routine with him, involving about as much emotion as brushing your teeth. Always the same with him, from Peking to Cairo."

"Sounds like setting-up exercises," Hardy said. He was running out of patience. He looked at me. "Can you dig up this girl for me, Mark?"

"I can give it a try," I said.

"I don't want a try, I want *her,*" Hardy said. "I can put cops on it if you don't care how much hell they raise with your peace and quiet."

"Do it, Mark," Chambrun said.

"We're just where we started," Hardy said. "An unknown girl in Hammond's bed; an unknown breakfast guest; an unknown killer. They can all be one and the same, or they can be three different people. Damn!"

CHAPTER THREE

It was approaching lunchtime, which is busy, busy, busy at the Beaumont. There's been a lot of political hoopla about three-martini lunches written off as business expenses. The Beaumont is where it's at.

The Trapeze Bar is on the mezzanine, a half floor up

from the main lobby. It is a very popular drinking spot, no food served except an enormous variety of hot and cold hors d'oeuvres. An artist of the Calder school had decorated it with little mobile circus figures operating on trapezes, which is where the room got its name. These mobiles are constantly in motion, thanks to an air-circulating system, which sucks off the fog of cigarette and cigar smoke. It is very bright and gay and charming, empty at noon, crowded at twelve-thirty.

I took Bobby Bryan with me on my search for Dorothy DeLavergne's girl friend. He was still pretty shaken up by what had happened.

"It's just not easy to take in," he said, as we walked down a flight of stairs to the mezzanine level and a side entrance to the Trapeze. "This girl isn't going to produce anything, you know."

"Oh?"

"She was with Geoff by eleven o'clock. Dorothy D. told me it would take half an hour for her friend to get there. She would have done her job and been on the way home by midnight. It never varied. What time did room service serve Geoff breakfast, do you know?"

"Eight o'clock, the order was for two. The waiter saw Hammond, who told him to leave the wagon and go. The same waiter came back a couple of hours later for the wagon and found Hammond dead."

"The girl had been gone eight hours when that breakfast was served," Bobby said.

"Maybe he talked to her, told her something that will give Hardy a lead."

"If he talked at all it was sex talk, to help stimulate him," Bobby said. "She won't have anything to help the police."

I turned and faced him just outside the door to the Trapeze. "You must have some ideas about what happened," I said.

"It's been going round and round in my head," he said, "and there's nothing."

"Conklin told us about this interview coming up with a Palestinian guy named Zadir," I said.

Bobby nodded. "Scheduled for tomorrow," he said. "We'll have to tell them it's off."

"Conklin suggested it may have been Israeli terrorists —Zionist hoodlums he called them—who didn't want that interview to happen."

"That's pretty far out," Bobby said. "Too much risk to stop what can't be too much trouble for them. Zadir has nothing new to talk about. Geoff has been all over it with him, and I was there to hear it. Pro-Palestinian, pro-Arab line from way back. You've heard it all, from Sadat on down."

"Private, personal enemies?" I asked.

He looked past me through the glass door to the Trapeze. The bar was filling rapidly with laughing, happy people. "Geoffrey was a cantankerous bastard," Bobby said. "I was fond of him, I loved my job with him, but I have to tell you what he was. In his work he got to know a great many things about a great many people that they didn't want him to know. He used those things, not just in his work, but to line his pockets and enhance his personal power in a power-hungry world. What was he like? He was a man interested in more money, more power, more wine, more women, more song, more power, more money. Does that describe him for you?"

"I guess."

"God knows who he had his knife in, twisting it and twisting it until he got what he wanted. Enemies? Countless, I'd say."

"You're telling me he was a professional blackmailer," I said.

Bobby shook his head as if he was remembering something with pleasure. "But nothing so crude as 'your money or your life,'" he said. "'I know something about you and if you don't turn over X bucks I'll make it public.' He moved important people around behind the scenes like a

30

master chess player. Sure, he had a reputation as a television journalist, but those people behind the scenes knew that he had far more power than that public exposure gave him. He was a genius at gratifying his own ego and getting paid for it in the bargain."

"So a lot of powerful people could have wished him dead," I said.

"It's ten to one that in a safe-deposit box somewhere in the world, probably Switzerland, there is evidence that will pay off the person who killed him. When the news of his murder breaks, Mark, dozens of world figures are going to be trembling in their boots. They may all go down the drain, whether they were involved in killing him or not. A good-sized earthquake in the offing."

"So, let's locate the girl if we can," I said.

"Waste of time," Bobby said.

I opened the door into the Trapeze and we were instantly greeted by a rumble of voices and laughter, which we couldn't hear out in the hall. Mr. Del Greco, the maitre d', who evidently had eyes in the back of his head, spotted us the moment we came in and gestured toward what appeared to be the only empty table in the room. There was a little "reserved" sign on it, but I knew it was reserved by Del Greco for his own friends.

"Early in the day for you, Mark," he said.

"Problems," I said. I could tell he didn't know about the situation in 3406. I introduced Bobby. "We're looking for a girl named Dorothy DeLavergne."

Del Greco raised a surprised eyebrow. The call girl situation in the Beaumont is handled as though it didn't exist. The girls, who patronize the various bars and restaurants in the hotel, are well known to the staff, but none of them would ever admit it. If, as a customer, you wanted to find yourself a woman and you asked—a bartender, a maitre d', a bellboy—you would be told politely that they couldn't help. But a few minutes later you would be approached, wherever you were, by what you were looking

31

for. To ask for a girl by name was not according to Hoyle.

I had Del Greco bend down so that people at the next table couldn't hear. "Not for publication," I said. "We have a homicide upstairs. The victim had a girl last night, sent to him by this Dorothy DeLavergne. He had asked for Dorothy but she was "otherwise engaged," to coin a phrase. The boss and the cops want to find the girl she sent."

Del Greco looked unhappy.

"The girl isn't suspected of anything," I said. "But she might be able to give Lieutenant Hardy some kind of lead."

Del Greco looked at Bobby. "You're Geoffrey Hammond's secretary, aren't you, Mr. Bryan?"

Bobby nodded.

"Is he the one?" Del Greco asked.

I said he was. Del Greco permitted himself a mild French oath.

"Big trouble," he said. He turned to survey the Trapeze, which was his kingdom. "Have a drink, gentlemen. I'll see what I can do."

I was brought up to believe that what my grandfather called "ladies of the evening" were "painted hussies," cheaply but suggestively dressed. My grandfather's image had them hanging around low-grade saloons, a cigarette dangling from scarlet lips, inching suggestively close to prospective customers. That image of the modern call girl must date back to the gold rush of forty-nine, eighteen forty-nine, that is.

In spite of her unlikely name, Dorothy DeLavergne looked like a nice, fresh, healthy Smith girl on her summer vacation. She wore little, if any, makeup; she had a nice summer tan. Her dark hair hung shoulder length, her dress was a simple cotton print. She could have been somebody's very pleasant sister, and probably was. She came over to our table less than one drink after Del Greco left us. Bobby and I both stood up to greet the lady. A waiter placed a chair for her. I found myself being looked over by candid dark eyes. I suspected she was an expert at making assessments of men.

"Del Greco says you want to talk to me, Mr. Haskell," she said. A pleasant husky voice.

"Hello, Dorothy," Bobby said. He'd had dealings with her, for Hammond, in the past.

"Del Greco told me about Mr. Hammond," she said. "My lucky night."

"Oh?" I said.

"I wasn't able to accept his invitation," she said. A nice way of putting it, I thought.

"But you sent someone to take your place," I said. "It's important that we locate her and talk to her."

"Loss of memory," Dorothy said.

"She's not in any trouble," I said. "From all accounts she was long gone when Hammond was attacked. But he might have said something to her, told her something; or she might have noticed or heard something, like a phone call."

"I wouldn't like to be fingered by someone if I were in her place," Dorothy said.

"Lieutenant Hardy, who's in charge of the case, understands that," I said. "That's why Bobby and I—not the police—are talking to you. Your friend may know absolutely nothing that will help, but they can't bypass her. If she would talk to me—"

Her dark eyes looked around the crowded room. "This place is going to explode when the news breaks," she said. "Anyone involved is going to make the headlines. If I tell you that will be bad for business, I think you'll understand, Mr. Haskell."

"If your friend won't make it difficult, she need never get any publicity," I said. "Mr. Chambrun wouldn't want it any more than she would."

She gave me a cheerful smile. "Your Mr. Chambrun doesn't want to deal with us but he can't do without us,"

33

she said. "We are an unmentionable part of his hospital-ity."

"Boys will be boys," I said.

She made up her mind. "Where and when?" she said briskly.

"My apartment. Two B on the second floor," I said. "As soon as possible."

She glanced at a plain gold wristwatch. "Half an hour?"

"Fine. What's her name?"

Again the cheerful smile. "That's up to her," she said. She stood up.

"Buy you a drink, Dorothy?" Bobby asked.

"I'll take a rain check, Bobby," she said, and disap-peared into the crowd, headed for a phone booth at the end of the room.

I reported to Hardy and he suggested I go on with it, so I headed for my apartment. Bobby had people he had to talk to, to notify that tomorrow's taping was off forever.

It couldn't have been more than twenty minutes and a cup of coffee after I'd gotten to my place when there was a knock on the door. Another "Smith girl" stood out in the hallway. The most distinctive thing about her was a classic black eye.

"Mr. Haskell?" she asked.

She was blond, the same fresh, young, unspoiled look about her as Dorothy—except for the shiner. I invited her in. She didn't seem reluctant. She looked around my liv-ing room, which is a hodgepodge of furniture styles, mementos of special events at the Beaumont, and photo-graphs of famous people I've managed to serve in some fashion, including Jack Kennedy, the late Joan Crawford, and dozens of others. I had a notion that my guest was an expert at sizing up strange rooms, learning something, quickly, about the men who occupied them.

"You have a name?" I asked her.

34

"Professionally, Sally Southern," she said. "It's not the name on my social security card."

"Coffee?"

"Black," she said.

I brought her a mug from the kitchenette, along with a fresh one for me. She was looking at the picture of a famous rock singer on my wall. She gave me a wry smile and I got the notion that he might have been a customer.

"Dorothy told me," she said. Her face hardened. "The sadistic bastard was all in one piece when I left him." She touched her eye, gingerly, with the tip of a forefinger. "I was warned that he liked to play rough, but it was an understatement. I got double the fee for this eye, because he had, at least, the decency to recognize that it would put me out of business for a couple of days."

She was so cool about her profession. I hadn't thought I could be turned off by it, but I was. I have always been absurdly romantic about my love life.

"Maybe we can begin with times," I said. "When you went to thirty-four-oh-six and when you left it."

She sipped her coffee. "Dorothy didn't tell me how it happened," she said.

"After he'd had breakfast with someone, served at eight o'clock, he was strangled from behind with a length of picture wire," I said.

"Oh, God!" she said. It was more politeness than shock.

"The first question the police asked was, were you his breakfast guest?" I said.

"The man is a quickie expert," she said. "I went to his room at a few minutes past eleven. I was home, bathing my eye, just a little after midnight."

"No proof of that, I suppose."

She gave me that wry smile again. "It may surprise you to hear that I live with two other girls," she said. "One or the other of them was at home all night. We come and go."

"I suppose," I said.

35

"It just happens they could testify for me if it was necessary."

"People who knew Hammond were certain you hadn't spent the whole night with him. Not his style, they said."

"Style! You know, Mr. Haskell, you run up against some awful creeps in this business. There are old guys who talk and talk and can't get anywhere. There are young guys who need teaching. And there are out-and-out sadists from whom you're lucky to escape in one piece. That was Hammond's ploy. Rip off your clothes, bang you around, a quick payoff and then you can't leave soon enough to please them."

"No preliminary conversation?"

"You're kidding," Sally Southern said. "I knocked on his door, he opened it, dragged me into the room, told me to go in the bedroom and take off my clothes."

"No phone calls?"

"One phone call," she said. "He made it. He told the switchboard operator not to put through any calls to him for an hour. He knew exactly how long it was going to take him!"

"He didn't mention anything about anyone he might be expecting after you left?"

"I tell you there was no conversation! About anything! He tore my dress when I wasn't ready for him quickly enough. When it was over he gave me twice the fee, four hundred clams. Plus taxi fare. I went down the fire stairs to the basement. My dress was in shreds. I called Mr. Cardoza, the maitre d' in the Blue Lagoon, on a house phone and he sent someone with a raincoat I could wear home. I couldn't go out on the street the way I looked."

"So Cordoza can also vouch for the time you left," I said. Cardoza is one of our good people.

She looked pleased, as though it hadn't occurred to her she could call on him for that kind of help.

36

"How do I reach you, Sally, in case Lieutenant Hardy wants more?"

She gave me a telephone number, which I wrote down. She smiled at me. "You don't have to keep it just for the police," she said.

"Thanks," I said. I knew I'd never call her for anything else.

My own telephone rang at that point. It was Betsy Ruysdale. She sounded strange, far away.

"Mark, you'd better get over here," she said. "We've got another one."

"Another what?"

"Picture-wire job," she said.

"What?"

"Joanna Fraser," Ruysdale said. "Room Sixteen fourteen. Same method, same result."

"Dead?"

"Very," Ruysdale said.

CHAPTER FOUR

I bustled little Miss Southern out of my place and hurried down the hall to Chambrun's office. I couldn't really take in what Ruysdale had told me. Another picture-wire job! Joanna Fraser!

Joanna Fraser was no "John Smith" at the Beaumont. She was a famous lady, though she might have slapped me down for calling her that. A famous "person" she'd have insisted. She was a big bell ringer for women's lib. Among other business activities, she was the publisher of *Liberation,* a magazine devoted to celebrating woman's escape from male domination. She financed a couple of fancy homes, one on the West Coast, for unwed mothers. She

37

was behind a very successful job-finding agency for women executives. She lectured up and down and across the country.

Joanna Fraser's father was MacDonald Fraser, who made it in oil, steel, railroads, airlines, and God knows what else. He left it all to Joanna, including a house in Newport, another in Palm Beach, and one in New York. At the time all this dropped into Joanna's lap she was married to Colin Dobler, a painter and sculptor of no particular distinction. The minute she came into her huge fortune Joanna mounted the platform of women's lib, took back her maiden name, kicked Colin Dobler out on his behind—but onto a very soft landing place. She provided him with a posh studio apartment on Gramercy Park, an allowance that gave him the look of a more than comfortably rich man, and maintained a room in each of her houses in case she needed him for whatever she might need him for. She sold the New York house, however, and bought a half-million-dollar co-op in the Beaumont. That was 1614. In our house chart 1614 was described as LR, DR, 2C, B, K, MR, P, or for you it meant living room, dining room, two chambers, boudoir, kitchen, maid's room, pantry. Rumor had it that the maid's room was kept for Colin Dobler, in case he was required to stay overnight. Maid service was supplied by the hotel, and at a maintenance fee of thirty-five-hundred dollars a month they could afford to supply it in style.

Joanna Fraser was, I guessed, in her early forties, handsome, always dressed to the nines, gay, almost neurotically verbal, determinedly devoted to her causes. A lot of women who like to use the title Ms. in front of their names were going to be very unhappy about her passing.

Others were going to be a lot unhappier, most notably Chambrun. Two murders in his hotel in the space of a few hours was a disaster. Two murders, giving all the indications that they'd been committed by the same person, suggested some kind of sick chain of violence that might still have a future.

Ruysdale's outer office was crowded with press people, among them my friend Dick Barrows. Two security men were blocking any kind of end run into Chambrun's office.

Barrows gave me a sardonic smile. "You didn't tell me there was going to be another one," he said.

"Nobody told me," I said.

"What the hell is going on?"

"I haven't caught up with it yet," I said. I had to fight off the others with a series of "no comments." What the hell, I had nothing to comment on yet.

I got through them and past the two security men into Chambrun's office. Ruysdale was there. Roy Conklin was still there, planted in that green leather armchair. He was parrying questions from Sergeant Baxter, one of Hardy's men. Baxter is a hard-nosed cop who takes no nonsense from anyone. I gathered he was trying to establish some connection between Geoffrey Hammond and Joanna Fraser. That would be an obvious police line, I knew. Chambrun and Hardy were both absent, undoubtedly up in 1614.

"My dear Sergeant," Conklin was saying in a weary voice, "I keep telling you Hammond didn't even know the Fraser woman."

"She was a personality," Baxter said. "Personalities were his business."

"He didn't know Elvis Presley, either," Conklin said. "Or the Beatles."

Ruysdale was standing by the west windows looking down at the park. I went over to her. She appeared to be as close to being rattled as I'd ever seen her.

"It's simply not believable," she said in a low voice. "Everything the same. There'd been someone there for a luncheon cocktail, which she'd made herself. No hotel service. Her chair tipped over backwards, wire around her neck. My God, Mark."

39

"Who found her?" I asked.

"Her secretary. Nora Coyle. You've seen her around. She has a key to the apartment."

I had not only seen Nora Coyle around, I'd made a few light-hearted passes at her in recent months. She was an extremely attractive brunette who didn't seem to have any permanent male appendages. I had supposed that might be a rule of the game if you worked for Joanna Fraser and her liberated allies. You mustn't seem to be any man's sex image. The modern woman is not supposed to be what women have always tried to be in the past.

"Rough for her," I said. "She has no explanation? No connection between Hammond and Joanna Fraser?"

"Nothing in a business or professional way," Ruysdale said. "The Coyle girl says Ms. Fraser had a social life that she kept very private. Not unnatural, maybe, since the other part of her life was so very public. Chambrun thinks Hardy's wasting his time trying to connect the two crimes."

"Same M.O.," I said.

"In the sense that there has to be a link between Hammond and Ms. Fraser. Each of them had some connection with the killer but not necessarily with each other. Look, Mark, you are to get to Mr. Wheaton at personnel. We need extra people."

"What kind of people?"

"To implement Security. Jerry Dodd has twenty men. We have forty floors, five hundred residence rooms, plus all the bars, restaurants, private rooms for private parties, kitchens, offices, God knows what else. Jerry's people can't begin to cover the whole territory."

"Cover?"

Ruysdale gave me a level look that had fear behind it. "Chambrun thinks we have a psycho on our hands, Mark. He thinks we can expect it to happen again."

The Man was thinking along the same lines I had. A sick chain of violence that might still have a future.

40

"How did this second thing get public?" I asked. "Your office is jammed with news people."

"The Coyle girl went screaming out into the corridor when she found Ms. Fraser," Ruysdale said. "A couple of guests were waiting for an elevator and went to help her. Before anyone could clamp down on them the word was out. There's going to be a run on the bank."

"How do you mean—run on the bank?"

"Front desk reports that transients are already starting to check out. Panic."

I can only imagine what it was like when the *Titanic*, the unsinkable ship, started to sink in midocean. I wasn't born then. What was happening in the Beaumont must have been more like the panic that swept the Bellevue-Stratford hotel in Philadelphia when news of the Legionnaires Disease spread. People wanted out, and in a hurry. It wasn't like a broken water main, or a fire, or some kind of violent private quarrel. You couldn't reassure people that it wouldn't happen again. The hell of it was that it could, and might. There was a madman on the loose and until we had him behind bars anyone could be his next target.

There is a private exit at the rear of Chambrun's office and I used it to avoid Dick Barrows and the other members of the fourth estate waiting in Ruysdale's office. From the mezzanine I took a look down at the main lobby. It was like the rush hour in the Times Square subway station, people jostling and crowding each other, a queue of them trying to get to the front desk to check out. People seemed to sense that there was safety in numbers. Nobody wanted to be left alone in an upstairs room. I had the uncomfortable feeling that a killer was watching this turmoil and enjoying it in his sick mind.

Later, when it was all over, I was impressed by the calm efficiency of Chambrun's staff. No one seemed to lose his or her head. No one left his post. The frightened people trying to check out were handled coolly and expertly by

41

the desk clerk and the cashiers. Some people just took off without bothering to check out or to pay their bills. The doormen and the bellboys helped them with their luggage, got them taxis. There were no arguments or debates. The bars were crowded and noisy. Again, the safety-in-numbers theory held. There is a fascination about being a spectator to violence if you don't feel in danger yourself.

My problem that early afternoon was that I'm a pretty well-known figure around the Beaumont. Most of the regulars are aware that I am a spokesman for management. If I went down into the lobby or into one of the crowded bars I'd never get away. I knew the back ways around the place, the fire stairs, the service elevators and corridors, and so I was able to get to the personnel office without being trapped by people hungry for the gory details.

Bill Wheaton, the personnel manager, was way ahead of me. He'd already been in touch with three major protection agencies. He'd come up with thirty-five men to augment our own security force. They were on their way.

"You know anything that makes any sense?" he asked me.

"Only what you know. Two people dead, one has to think killed by the same freak."

"No leads?"

"I haven't caught up with the second one yet," I said.

Bill is a pleasant, sandy-haired, breezy guy who is very shrewd in his judgments of people. That's why he has the job of hiring the help. "If I had Jerry Dodd's job, which thank God I do not," he said, "I'd be thinking very hard about this Frazer woman's husband—or ex-husband. I hear rumors, you know. What's his name? Dobler? The maids on sixteen tell me they'd had some pretty loud screaming fights. Knock-down-and-drag-out."

"You're suggesting Colin Dobler—?"

"Why not?" Bill said cheerfully. "I read statistics somewhere. Seventy-five percent of all homicides in the United States are the result of family quarrels!"

"So he killed Geoffrey Hammond first just to practice up?" I asked.

Bill grinned at me. "Man has to perfect his skills," he said. "You catching up with Jerry Dodd? I haven't been able to get him on the phone."

"My next stop is sixteen," I said.

"Tell him I'll have extra men for him here any minute, but someone else will have to brief them on what they're expected to do."

They were expected to protect more than a thousand resident guests and God knows how many hundreds of in-and-outs from a strangler's wire. But how?

For the first time in my experience Chambrun and Lieutenant Walter Hardy were at odds. Hardy, the methodical one, confronted with two murders, was proceeding as though they were routine. He was trying to build up a picture of the lives of the victims, their relationships with people, searching for a motive. By the time he was done there would be detailed dossiers on Geoffrey Hammond and Joanna Fraser, on their relatives, friends, business associates, rivals, on truths about them, rumors about them. When all these details were carefully collected, Hardy would sit down in front of them, like a jigsaw wizard, and put them together into a finished picture. Combine this with whatever tangible evidence the professionals could dig up and you might have an answer. Today? Tomorrow? Next week? Whenever, it would be solid, it would be firm, it would hold.

Chambrun couldn't wait for that "whenever." Two guests in his hotel had been murdered within a space of four or five hours. The waiter who had served Hammond's breakfast for two had seen Hammond alive at eight that morning and found him dead at ten. Nora Coyle, Joanna Fraser's secretary, had seen her employer alive at eleven o'clock that morning, gone out to do some errands, and found her dead at a quarter past one. The two murders had taken place three to four hours apart. Chambrun's concern was not a wrapped-up case for the district attorney.

"If a madman follows this cockeyed pattern," Chambrun was saying to Hardy when I joined them in 1614, "we can look for him to strike again about four o'clock this afternoon!"

"We can only just keep digging," Hardy said patiently.

"Digging my foot!" Chambrun said. "I am only concerned with protecting my guests, my friends, my staff. You sit here, Walter, dusting this room for fingerprints and getting a history from ex-husbands and secretaries and business associates, while a psychotic killer may already have selected his next target, could be moving in on it as we stand here arguing."

The man with the long hairdo in the far corner of the room must be, I thought, Colin Dobler, Joanna Fraser's husband or ex-husband. He looked like a man in a trance. The lovely Nora Coyle was sitting beside a police stenographer equipped with a tape recorder. She'd evidently been making some sort of statement when Chambrun had blown his top. Jerry Dodd was involved with some police technicians. There was an overturned armchair, but Joanna Fraser's body had been removed. Chalk marks on the rug indicated where it had been found.

"What is it you think I should be doing?" Hardy asked patiently.

"We need protection!" Chambrun said.

"Five-hundred-odd suites and rooms and special assembling places—bars, restaurants, the works," Hardy said. "You're asking for an army I haven't got, Pierre."

Chambrun brought his fist down on the back of a chair behind which he was standing. "Where will he strike next? That's the answer I want. Getting statements from people who won't tell you the truth if they're guilty

44

isn't going to do us a damn bit of good!"

"The news is out," Hardy said. "It's on every television and radio station. There isn't a person in this hotel, coming or going, who doesn't know what's happened. That's protection in itself, Pierre. No one is going to be careless."

"If this sick bastard is just killing at random, Walter, no one is going to suspect that he is the next target. That in itself is a carelessness. There is no time to warn people, no time to make a convincing public statement."

"I repeat, Pierre, what do you want me to do that I can do?" Hardy asked.

"Goddamn it, Walter, if I had the answer to that I wouldn't be standing here talking."

"It's possible that there's no connection between these two crimes," Hardy said, "in spite of the identical method. It can be a psycho, as you suggest, just killing for the pleasure of it. But it's also possible that there is a connection. If there is, it would help us protect the next intended victim—if there is one. That's what I have to stay with, Pierre. I'll get you as many men as I can to help, but it will only be a handful, and I'm afraid I don't think it will be the slightest bit of help if you're right about the nature of the killer. He'll simply strike where no one is watching, and we can't possibly watch everywhere."

I managed to interrupt. I told Chambrun that Bill Wheaton had thirty-five extra guards on the way.

"You could empty the hotel," Hardy said quietly. "You would if it were a bomb."

There are plans, techniques, set up for evacuating the hotel in case of a major emergency, like an all-consuming fire, a serious bomb threat, or the possibility of an enemy air raid. There are plans for evacuating portions of the hotel. But none of them are as simple as pressing a button and, presto, the hotel is empty of people. People, up to a few thousand, bewildered, frightened, have to be moved. They would, I suspect, become like cattle in a burning barn. Their personal stalls would appear to be the safest place. They would, quite literally, have to be prodded out. No matter how efficient the staff, the resulting panic would lead to unbelievable confusion.

I could almost hear those thoughts revolving in Chambrun's mind as he stared steadily at Hardy. Such a happening in the Beaumont would be to him like painting graffiti on the walls of a church would be to a priest.

"If it was a bomb," he said to Hardy very quietly, the anger gone out of his voice, "we would locate it, clear the area, and get experts to deactivate it. When that was done the place would be safe and people could come back to it. This is different. We can push people out onto the streets, keep them there for hours, days, weeks, and if we haven't nailed this monster, it will be just as dangerous for them to come back as it is for them to stay here now. This bastard has chosen the Beaumont as his playground. We will only catch him *in* it. After you have sifted all the statements and counterstatements, you may have a lead. It's my fear that he'll move again before you reach that point. Our best chance is to catch him when he makes that move. The people best equipped for that are those on my staff, who will know when someone is in some place he has no business to be. You go to your church, friend, and I'll go to mine."

He turned and walked out of the room, but he called me from the foyer. He was standing there, lighting a cigarette, when I joined him.

"I'm going to prepare a statement for all the resident guests of the hotel," he said, "telling them that there is a lunatic loose. We'll do our best to protect them. They can stay or go as they choose. I'll arrange a statement to be broadcast in all the public rooms, and something for television and radio. People will be warned and can make their own decisions."

"You'll need me to help you with that," I said.

"No, Mark." He took a deep drag on his cigarette. "I

46

understand you're friends with the Coyle girl." He nodded toward the living room.

"We've had a few drinks together."

"Talk to her when Hardy's finished with her. If she isn't under pressure, she may spill something she doesn't realize she's been holding back. You obviously have special charms for most ladies."

"I'll talk to her," I said.

"And cultivate Bobby Bryan when you can," he said. "When Hardy stops asking them where they were at the time of the murder, they may come up with something helpful."

"But if the killer is just choosing people at random—?"

"I don't really believe in that," Chambrun said. "There is a connection of sorts. It may not be rational, it may not make sense to anyone but the killer. But it's a pattern he's dreamed up out of something. Hammond's people say Hammond didn't know Joanna Fraser. Ms. Fraser's secretary and her ex-husband say she didn't know Hammond. But there has to be someplace where they touch the same base. See if you can smell it out, Mark. Because there may be a third person who touches that base, and if there is, he or she is marked down as the killer's next victim."

"I'm not an expert at that kind of questioning," I said.

"You're an expert at listening," he said. "That's your special gift, Mark. Get them talking—and listen as you've never listened before."

I had never really thought of myself as a listener. My job is to sell the hotel, which means talking and writing—giving out. But Chambrun had seen another aspect, the listening part of it: listening to complaints, listening to people who try to con us one way or the other. My judgments of people from what they had to say to me was important to management. I hadn't thought of that very seriously before now. It was flattering that Chambrun saw a value in me I hadn't considered.

The actors had moved to new positions when I went back into the living room. Hardy had disappeared, along with Jerry Dodd and the police technicians. I could hear their voices down the hall where they were obviously going over the other rooms in Joanna Fraser's luxurious pad.

The police stenographer had fitted Nora Coyle with a headset so that she could listen to her own statement on the tape recorder.

Colin Dobler, the ex-husband artist, was standing so close to the entrance that I wondered if he'd been trying to listen to my conversation with Chambrun. A closer look told me that this was a far from unattractive man. Men in their early fifties with long hair tend to turn me off. I don't think I have any particular prejudice against long hair, but it has seemed to me to be a symbol of the very young, and when older men choose to go that way they seem to be reaching for an irretrievable past.

But there was nothing affected about Dobler. He had obviously been taken away, hurriedly, from whatever his daily routine was. His tan summer-weight slacks were paint stained, as was his pale yellow sports shirt, open at the throat. He'd put on a clean corduroy jacket. I got the feeling he'd been painting in his Gramercy Park studio when the word came.

He had pleasant brown eyes, a relaxed mouth, and a low, easy voice when he spoke. He could, I thought, be attractive to women, which explained why Joanna Fraser hadn't been willing to let him go entirely, even after they had split.

"It's just not possible to take in," he said to me. "I saw her and I don't believe it."

"Shocking for you," I said.

"My God, for anyone who saw her," he said. "She was a beautiful woman suddenly transformed into a grotesque

48

horror. She was—was frightened of growing old, frightened of death, but this is beyond anything she could have thought of in her wildest nightmares."

"Two in one day is a little hard for any of us to take," I said. "I'm told she was apparently having cocktails with someone."

He nodded. "She prided herself on her extra-dry martinis," he said. "That's what she made for this butcher, whoever he is."

"Nora—Miss Coyle—doesn't know who she was expecting for a drink? The time suggests it was a drink before going to lunch with someone."

"Joanna had no formal appointment," Dobler said. "But coming in here was like coming through a revolving door. Joanna prepared for the day very carefully—bathing, makeup, dressing. She kept all that very private, even from her husband—when I was working at it. But after juice and coffee she belonged to the world, to anyone who knocked on her door. People in the women's movement came and went like characters on a merry-go-round. Joanna would listen to anyone's gripes. It didn't have to be a friend she made drinks for; it could have been for anyone who turned up at the cocktail time. She was a very private woman in her private life, and very public the rest of the time."

"What concerns us at the moment is to find some connection with Geoffrey Hammond," I said. "Two violences exactly alike—"

He shook his head. He was fumbling in his pocket for a pipe, which he began to fill from an oilskin pouch. A very relaxed man in spite of what had happened.

"I couldn't help overhearing your conversation with Mr. Chambrun," he said.

He couldn't help it if he had moved over to the doorway to listen, I thought.

"I was very close to Joanna, though we were technically separated," he said. He held a lighter to his pipe and puffed out a mildly aromatic cloud of smoke. "There was nothing wrong with our marriage except the Cause."

"The Cause?" I said.

"Women's lib," he said. "When she came into her money she went haywire. She insisted on taking back her maiden name; she insisted on separate domiciles. She made a great public display of those moves. But privately —well, I was still her lover, Mr. Haskell. All she had to do was beckon, and I was here, there, wherever she wanted me to be. What I'm trying to say is that we remained intimate, close. She talked to me about everything that mattered to her; talked to me as she would not have talked to anyone else. I've been trying to remember, since Lieutenant Hardy first spoke to me, if there was ever anything at all about Geoffrey Hammond."

"And was there?"

"Only one very small meaningless thing," he said. "One night when I was staying here—oh, I spent nights here, Mr. Haskell. I was expected to spend nights when she wanted me, to reassure her that she was still an 'old-fashioned' woman, in spite of her public insistence that she was a 'new' woman."

And he responded because she kept him, I thought. He made love to her for money. Perhaps that wasn't fair. Perhaps he really cared about her. Was there a way to know which it was?

"As I was saying, one small meaningless thing. Hammond was interviewing Henry Kissinger on television and we had the set turned on. A little into the program Joanna said to me, 'What an insufferable ego!' I said something to the effect that that was Kissinger's style. 'I'm not talking about Kissinger,' Joanna said. 'That jerk, Hammond!' That is the only time I can remember Hammond being mentioned. She certainly had no professional dealings with him, no private social life that involved him. As far as I know she had never met him or talked to him. She could have, of course, at some public function or in some public place. It could have been no more than a public introduction. Her mention of him that night was no more important than if you or I had said we didn't like an actor in a certain part. It wasn't a personal thing."

"If you heard Chambrun, you know he thinks there must have been some base that they touched mutually," I said. "I think he meant, for example, that they both contributed to the Red Cross, or to Jimmy Carter's campaign fund, or were both opposed to some piece of legislation. The same base, without knowing each other or being involved together."

"So far as I know, Hammond never interviewed anyone connected with women's lib," Dobler said. "The only legislation Joanna concerned herself with was equal rights for women. I don't know where Hammond stood on that. Probably they both did contribute to the Red Cross, along with millions of other people. But anything that would account for this incredible kind of slaughter, no! They simply didn't know each other."

"It doesn't have to be something that would account for it in our minds," I said, "only in the killer's mind. All we know about his mind is that it's twisted out of shape."

At that point Hardy reappeared from down the hall. He stopped by Nora Coyle and the police stenographer. She was just removing the headset from her soft dark hair. The stenographer had turned off the tape recorder.

"You satisfied with it, Miss Coyle?" Hardy asked. "Want to change anything?"

"No," Nora said. "You asked me for facts and I've given them to you."

"It'll be transcribed and then you can sign it," Hardy said. "But I need you where I can find you, Miss Coyle. New things will keep coming up. You and Mr. Dobler are our only sources for double checking."

"Do I have to stay here?" Nora asked, her voice not steady.

I realized that she meant this apartment. She was apparently occupying one of the bedrooms down the hall.

"Certainly not in this suite," Hardy said. "We have a lot to check out here." He glanced at me. "Maybe Mark can find you another room somewhere in the hotel."

"From all accounts there may be hundreds of them available," I said.

"I'd be very grateful, Mark," Nora said. "I'll get a few things from my room."

She took off down the hall.

"Pierre going to close up shop?" Hardy asked me.

"I don't think so," I said. "He's going to get warnings to everyone but leave it up to them. He thinks—"

"I know what he thinks," Hardy said. He drew a deep breath and turned to Colin Dobler. He gestured toward the tape machine. "It's your turn, Mr. Dobler."

CHAPTER FIVE

I think it was Noel Coward who said that no matter what a man and woman appear to be talking about on stage, they are really talking about sex.

Before that afternoon Nora Coyle and I had been involved in a rather casual fencing match. She knew what I wanted. Being rather expert at the game, she played it so well that I wasn't sure whether she was going to say yes in the end or not. I guess I am old fashioned. Kids today just say to the girl, 'Will you?' and if the girl says no they go whistling off down the block to find someone else to ask. I enjoy the preliminaries. I'm not so hungry that I'm partial to one-night stands. I have said somewhere before that I am inclined to fall in love forever every six months. I guess I play the game in the hope that the show will have some sort of a run after opening night.

That afternoon was no time to think of game-playing with Nora. But I am a sinister bastard, come to think of it. Kindness and sympathy at this moment of shock might pay dividends in the long run. I would even be doing my job for Chambrun in the process. So much for my image as a white knight.

Nora reappeared with a small traveling case, which I took from her.

"Let me know where I can reach you, Miss Coyle," Hardy said.

Nora and I walked out into the hall and to the elevators. The moment we were out of Hardy's sight she was hanging onto my arm as if her life depended on it.

"I'm going to take you to my apartment," I said. She'd been there before. She had, in effect, seen my etchings and survived. "There'll be a drink, or coffee, or whatever you need. From there I'll try to locate a place for you. To go down to the lobby right now is to walk into the middle of a riot."

She nodded. She was fighting tears and suddenly she lost the battle. She clung to me, sobbing, as we waited for the elevator. By some miracle we inherited an empty car on the way down. We got off at two and I herded her down the hall to my place. There she collapsed in an armchair, still weeping.

She drank Scotch, I knew, and I fixed her a moderately stiff drink with soda. She took a sip of it, choked on it, put it down on the table beside the chair, and went back to fighting the torrent of tears. I pretended to be looking for something at my desk across the room. Suddenly I saw her bang her fists down on the arms of the chair.

"I've got to stop this foolishness!" she almost shouted.

"Why?" I said, drifting back to her. "Do you good." I handed her my handkerchief.

She gave me a ghastly smile through her tears. "Scene from a movie," she said, and blew her nose—in my handkerchief. Then: "Oh God, Mark, I found her. I saw her, you know."

I nodded. "Don't tell me. I saw Hammond."

"Was it—was he—"

"Just the same, from all accounts."

"She never hurt anyone in the world, except herself, and maybe Colin," Nora said.

"Try your drink," I said. "It could work magic."

She drank, and the hurricane of tears seemed to abate. "Can you imagine walking in there and—seeing her—like that?"

"Rough," I said. I went over to the kitchenette and made myself a drink. It was early in the day for me, but I decided I needed one, and she needed time to get in complete control. I have to say one thing for Nora. She looked pretty damned appetizing even when she'd been crying.

It all came out of her now, in a flood of words. "I've worked for her now for six years," she said.

"You must have started awfully young."

"I'm twenty-six, if that kind of statistic interests you, Mark."

"You've aged well," I said.

She shook her head as if to say she wasn't interested in that kind of game. "A whole new world for me," she said. "Travel—every place you can imagine in this country and Europe. I'd never booked a plane flight in my life, and suddenly I was a travel expert. But it was different from anything I'd known. An all-woman world. She really believed in it, you know."

"Not enough to have done anything about it until she had the money to play the role," I said.

"You've been talking to Colin," she said.

"Not about that," I said.

"I have to admit he got the short end of the stick," she said. "She couldn't front for the liberation movement and be a happily married woman."

54

"But she kept him in her bed," I said. "And he came whenever she whistled. For the money?"

"I think he really loves her." She caught her breath. "Loved her. He took what she gave him in order to stay close to what he wanted."

"Were they legally divorced or just playing that game for her public?"

"Legally divorced," Nora said. "The record had to be clear in case somebody wanted to check up on her." She hesitated, frowning. "He's a very rich man now. She willed him a big chunk of her estate."

"If you told Hardy that, it'll make Colin a pretty solid suspect."

"Hardy didn't ask me that."

"If he had, and you told him, his next question would be what did Colin have against Geoffrey Hammond?"

"I never heard either of them mention Hammond," Nora said. "I don't think Joanna knew him or was concerned about him in any way."

"Chambrun thinks there must be some connection between them."

"I don't know what it could be." She paused again, with that little-girl frown marring her forehead. "I used to watch some of his interviews on television. Joanna didn't think much of him as an interviewer. Joanna thought he was always trying to sell himself instead of the person he was talking to. But she never indicated that she knew him or had ever had any contact with him. What could it be, Mark?"

"You've got me," I said.

She emptied her glass and put it down on the side table. "I'm confronted with something pretty unpleasant," she said. "This morning I had a job, a future, a well-organized life. Right now I don't know where I go next."

"You shouldn't have any problems," I said.

"You think not?" She gave me a bitter little smile. "If your policeman doesn't solve this case in a hurry, everyone connected with Joanna will be a suspect in the public eye. Colin. Me. No one is going to hire a girl who might be a strangler."

"Bull," I said.

"Think about it."

"All right. I've thought about it. I don't buy it."

Again that bitter little smile. "Fine. You got a job for me?"

"Could be. How about another drink?"

"I might as well be potted as the way I am," she said, and handed me her glass.

"It's hard to believe that this could happen to anyone," she said, as I was building her drink.

"It's happened to all of us," I said.

"Not to you," she said. "Would you believe this is the second time I've been in the same place with a strangler who used picture wire to do the job?"

I felt a strange little chill run down my spine. "What the hell are you talking about?" I asked. I handed her the fresh drink.

"The Sharon Dain case," she said, not looking at me.

"Who is Sharon Dain?"

She looked up at me. "Don't you remember, Mark, a couple of years ago, in a ski resort in High Crest, Colorado? The girl who strangled her lover with picture wire? It was the hot story of the day."

It came back to me out of a dim past. Some tootsie living with a ski instructor someplace in Colorado. She'd strangled the guy. I didn't recall the picture-wire detail. The girl had some big-name friends in the movie colony who tried to help her, but she was convicted of murder one, as I recalled it.

"What have you got to do with this Sharon Dain?" I asked.

"Not anything, except that I was there when it happened."

"In Colorado?"

56

"High Crest," she said. "It's a fancy resort. One of Joanna's liberation groups was holding a convention there when it happened. It was pretty shocking. I mean, we'd seen Sharon Dain and her boyfriend around in the evenings. Glamorous and something of a local scandal."

"And she killed him with picture wire?"

Nora nodded.

"So everybody else at High Crest was connected with it just the way you were—which is not at all," I said.

"I was connected a little more than some," she said. "You remember an up-and-coming young movie star named Lance Wilson?"

It was a name I couldn't put a face to.

"He came to me for help," Nora said.

"Why you?"

"Because I was Joanna's secretary. He wanted Joanna's help. A lone woman being persecuted by male police, a male district attorney, a predominantly male community. That, Wilson thought, would be Joanna's meat. He persuaded me to go to the local jail to see Sharon Dain."

"And you, soft-hearted sucker, went?"

"Yes. I had to have facts if I was going to get any help from Joanna. And it was better to get them from Sharon herself than from her lawyer."

"Oh, brother!" I said.

"Sharon Dain was a very beautiful, very sexy, very desperate girl," Nora said. "She told me her ski instructor boyfriend—his name was Harold Carpenter—was a sadistic monster. He beat her up, threatened her life. In the middle of one of his sadistic orgies she strangled him to save her own life."

"She drew her trusty picture wire and shot him down?"

"Something like that."

"And you bought it?"

"I took it to Joanna, in any case."

"And she?"

"Wouldn't touch it. She told me, quite sensibly, that

57

women's liberation didn't mean the freedom to commit murder. She got an anonymous threatening letter from someone after I told Lance Wilson she wouldn't help."

"Where is Sharon Dain now?"

"In prison—I think. She got a stiff sentence after she was convicted. As I remember, it would have been twelve to fifteen years before she'd be eligible for parole."

It was far out, but a picture-wire killer had crossed Joanna Fraser's path in the past.

"I think maybe we better go down the hall and talk to Chambrun," I said to Nora.

Ruysdale was at her desk in the outer office when Nora and I got there. I wondered where the press and media people were who'd jammed up the place earlier, and learned that Chambrun, in spite of a storm of protest, had barred them from the second floor. Our security people were sealing off thirty-four, sixteen, and here. They couldn't have been doing much about looking for a crazy man with a roll of picture wire in his pocket.

"Nora has come up with something interesting I think the boss should hear," I said.

Ruysdale gave Nora a sympathetic look. "There just isn't anything very comforting to say, Miss Coyle," she said. I guess she saw that any kind of sweet talk would loosen the floodgates again. She picked up the phone on her desk. "Mark and Miss Nora Coyle to see you, Mr. Chambrun." Then she waved toward the far door.

"How is the general climate?" I asked her.

"Warnings are out," Ruysdale said. "They seem to have turned the tide. People not so anxious to leave. They're like motorists rubbernecking at an accident."

Chambrun was at his desk. His exterior never showed any signs of his been ruffled. He knew I wouldn't be here with Nora unless she had something that might interest him.

"Please sit down, Miss Coyle," he said, gesturing to the armchair beside his desk.

"It's a coincidence that may not mean anything," I said.

"Most coincidences don't," he said. "However, let's hear it."

Nora, in pretty good control now, told her story of the Sharon Dain case and Joanna Fraser's connection with it. Chambrun listened, his eyes narrowed in those deep pouches. He didn't interrupt or ask her anything. When she'd finished he picked up his phone and spoke to Ruysdale.

"Get Roy Conklin or Bobby Bryan in here," he said; "whichever can move fastest." He put down the phone and lit one of his flat cigarettes. "You mentioned an anonymous threat, Miss Coyle."

"It was a letter, written on High Crest stationery," she said, "available to hundreds of people, Mr. Chambrun, the way Hotel Beaumont stationery is available to any guests here."

"Do you remember what it said?"

"Just a sentence," Nora said. " 'You will pay for your indifference to Sharon Dain.' "

"No signature?"

"No."

"And that was two years ago? Nothing since?"

"Not that I know of." Nora twisted in her chair. "Anonymous threats and slanderous attacks weren't unusual. I guess most public people get them. Joanna ignored them."

"She wasn't afraid?"

"Joanna wasn't afraid of God himself," Nora said with a little smile.

"She should have been, it seems," Chambrun said. "I think Hardy should be in on this." He had Ruysdale connect him with 1614. While he waited for Hardy to come on he spoke to Nora. "You didn't mention all this in the statement you gave Hardy?"

"I hadn't even thought of it until Mark and I got to talking," Nora said. "I mean, it was two years ago, and what happened today was so immediate. I wasn't thinking of anything else when Lieutenant Hardy questioned me."

Hardy came on and Chambrun said, "I may have something, Walter."

While he waited, Chambrun proceeded to make a series of phone calls from a list on the desk in front of him. I recognized the people he was calling as permanent residents of the hotel, mostly co-op apartment owners and old friends and customers. He had a set speech for them, telling what had happened, what the risks were. They were not to let anyone into their rooms, not even maids, or waiters, or bellboys, until the coast was clear.

"You suspect someone on the staff?" I asked him between calls.

"I suspect someone posing as someone on the staff," he said. "Both Hammond and Joanna Fraser were unprepared for any sort of attack. They wouldn't have suspected a waiter, or a maid, or a maintenance man who managed to get behind them, ostensibly doing some routine job."

He went on with his calling until Hardy walked in.

The detective listened to Nora's story, frowning. "It provides some sort of remote motive," he said when she'd finished. "But what, if any, is the connection with Hammond?"

"Let's see," Chambrun said. The light was blinking on his phone and he picked it up. "Send him in," he said to Ruysdale.

Bobby Bryan, Hammond's secretary, joined us. Chambrun introduced him to Nora.

"We both seem to be out of a job, Miss Coyle," Bobby said. Then, to Chambrun, "What's up?"

"You ever hear of the Sharon Dain case?" Chambrun asked.

"Sure," Bobby said promptly. "Gal who strangled her boyfriend at some ski resort in Colorado." He stopped, his eye widening. "With picture wire!"

60

"Interesting, no?" Chambrun said. "Tell me, Bryan, were you and Hammond out in High Crest, Colorado, when that happened?"

"Good God, no," Bobby said. "I've never been to Colorado. Neither had Hammond in the ten years I was with him."

"And Hammond had no connection with the Dain case?"

"No. That is, he refused to have a connection."

"How do you mean?"

Bobby shrugged. "The Dain girl had stirred up a lot of support for herself among the guests out there. They got Max Steiner, one of the most famous and expensive defense lawyers in the country, to handle the Dain girl's case. He called Hammond, long distance to New York, with a crazy proposal. He wanted Hammond to interview Sharon Dain on TV. His case was to be self-defense while the girl was driven to legal insanity by her boyfriend's sadistic treatment. Max Steiner wanted to make his case to the whole world and not just to a jury."

Chambrun was almost smiling. "And Hammond refused?"

"Sure. In spite of a whopping fee Steiner offered. Hammond felt he was being used, and nobody ever used Geoffrey Hammond."

Chambrun leaned back in his chair, and his smile had reached Cheshire-cat proportions. "So there's the base they both touched without either of them knowing it," he said. "They both refused to help Sharon Dain." The smile evaporated. "The next question is, who else refused? Someone who may be staying here in the Beaumont?"

Part Two

CHAPTER ONE

Lieutenant Hardy was on the phone to High Crest, Colorado, almost before Chambrun had finished speaking. Nothing so obvious as an escaped Sharon Dain, out to massacre all the people who refused to help her in her time of trouble, developed. Colorado police assured Hardy that Sharon Dain was safely tucked away in a state prison for women. She hadn't escaped. She wasn't even due for a parole hearing for another ten years. She had, it seemed, through her lawyer, Max Steiner, moved to appeal her conviction on technical grounds involving her trial, and had been turned down by the state's highest court. That final decision had been handed down just about a month ago.

"You might think the woman's lover was out on some kind of revenge kick," Hardy said, "except that she killed her lover—with picture wire!"

"She killed *that* lover with picture wire," Chambrun said. He looked around at the rest of us. "Who knows anything about this Dain girl except for the murder case?"

No one spoke.

"You, Miss Coyle," Chambrun said, "were approached by an actor named Lance Wilson to get help from Joanna Fraser."

Nora nodded. I could see she was trying to put together memories of something almost forgotten.

"He had just had a big success playing a supporting role to a major star," she said. "I can't remember—Kirk Douglas, Burt Lancaster, somebody like that. He is young, in his early twenties, I'd guess. The Dain girl must be ten years older."

"Maybe he liked older women," Chambrun said. "I did at that age. What's become of him?"

"I don't think he's had anything big," Nora said. "I see him on TV dramas from time to time. But I don't think—"

"What don't you think, Miss Coyle?"

"The situation at High Crest was rather special," she said. "High Crest is a ski resort, but it's more like a private club. The same people come back year after year, or friends of those same people come. They book most of the accommodations well in advance. There isn't ever much room for the general public."

"Just what point does that make?" Chambrun asked.

"Everybody knew everybody," Nora said. "Everybody was rich, or friends with someone rich."

"But you were there for a convention."

"Joanna could afford to buy space anywhere she wanted. If she needed a friend in court she had one."

"So everybody was well off. The Dain girl?"

"I don't think so."

"She hired the most expensive defense lawyer in the country."

"I think friends put up the money for her."

"What friends?"

"I don't know, Mr. Chambrun. The only friend I met was Lance Wilson. Somehow I didn't think he was a friend

66

in the sense that we use the word. It was more that he was on her side."

"I'm afraid you're confusing me, Miss Coyle," Chambrun said.

"Everyone knew Harold Carpenter, the man who was murdered," Nora said. "He'd been a ski instructor at High Crest for a number of years. A dark, handsome man with a beautiful athletic body. A kind of noisy glamor boy." She lowered her eyes. "The Dain girl lived in his cabin, but that didn't reduce his interest in other attractive women. I think—I think he brought Sharon Dain to High Crest. The management would have permitted him to have any guest he chose. He was important to them."

So our Nora had battled with Harold Carpenter, I thought. I hoped he'd had no better luck than I'd had.

"The people at High Crest seemed to take sides after Carpenter was murdered," Nora said. "I don't mean that there were people who were Sharon Dain's friends—who loved her. She was—in my opinion—a cheap, rather gaudy little tramp. The division was over Harold Carpenter. Some people thought he was marvelous; some people thought he was a jerk. Those who thought he was a jerk believed Sharon Dain's story of sadism and violence. They accepted her story that she'd acted in self-defense. The others adored Carpenter and thought Sharon should get the works."

"A question," Hardy interrupted. "How can you sneak up behind a man, strangle him with picture wire when he's off guard, and call it self-defense?"

Nora seemed to be having trouble keeping her voice steady. "Those on Sharon's side believed Carpenter was capable of all kinds of perverted violence," she said. "Max Steiner, her lawyer, contended that she was a prisoner in Carpenter's cabin; that in a lull between violences she chose the only possible way she could to escape him. Her supporters bought that. I think Lance Wilson was one of them. They formed a defense committee and I've always thought they paid the bills."

I noticed Ruysdale going through the phone book. She marked a place with her forefinger. "I have Max Steiner's phone number," she said.

Chambrun gave her a special little smile I'd seen there before. It signaled his appreciation of Ruysdale's ability to be one step ahead of his demands.

"Please," he said. Then, as Ruysdale went out to her own office, "Max Steiner can at least tell us who did pay his bill, which, with appeals and all, must have been quite something."

"From what I know of him," Hardy said sourly, "he won't talk to you without a consultation fee."

The lieutenant proved to be wrong. Almost at once the red light blinked on Chambrun's phone. He turned on the squawk box and picked up the receiver.

"I have Mr. Steiner on the line," Ruysdale said.

"Mr. Steiner?" Chambrun said.

A brisk, energetic voice came through to us. I'd seen pictures of Steiner and knew him to be a small, wiry, grey powerhouse. "I had a feeling someone in your world might be trying to reach me, Mr. Chambrun," he said.

"Oh?"

Steiner laughed. "Not everybody in the world has the dubious pleasure of being involved with strangling-by-picture-wire."

"I have you on an open line, Mr. Steiner. Lieutenant Hardy of Homicide is here, also a member of my staff; my secretary, and a young woman who was Joanna Fraser's secretary. You've heard the news from here?"

"Yes. I don't mind an audience, Mr. Chambrun. I'm at my best with an audience."

"We've made a strange connection with the Dain case," Chambrun said. "It seems that both our victims, Geoffrey Hammond and Joanna Fraser, had a similar involvement with Sharon Dain. They both refused to help her."

"I know," Steiner said. "I knew at the time. I was sitting

here wondering if I should tell someone that when your call came."

"You think there's some significance in that?"

"I don't know enough about your end of it to make a guess," Steiner said. "But if I were you I'd certainly be wondering."

"So then you'll understand my first question. Who paid your fees, Mr. Steiner?"

"You won't believe it," Steiner said.

"Try me."

"I don't know," Steiner said. He laughed again. "I have been paid over two hundred thousand dollars for the first trial and for the appeals, and I don't know who paid it."

"It is hard to believe. I understand there was some kind of defense committee. I thought they—"

"Oh, there was a committee, and they hired me. They, technically, paid me. But the money came from an anonymous source."

"I don't understand."

"There was a man out there named Parker, Alvin Parker. He's president of the Parker Foundation. They give away millions of dollars to the arts every year. He was chairman of that committee. He approached me. I told him what a defense was likely to cost. He didn't know how to raise it."

"With millions at his command?" Chambrun asked. He was making some kind of signals to Ruysdale, who was standing in the far doorway. It suddenly came to me in that moment. The Parker Foundation was giving some kind of a fund-raising do in the Grand Ballroom that night. Alvin Parker was a guest in the hotel!

"Alvin Parker is the nephew of Joshua Parker, the oil billionaire, who created the Parker Foundation in his will. Alvin Parker is, no doubt, well off. But he doesn't have a free hand with the foundation money. It has to go to the arts. Perhaps, if Sharon Dain had been an artist, the foundation could have justified some sort of contribution to her defense. But she wasn't that kind of artist."

"What kind of artist was she?"

Steiner chuckled. "In bed," he said.

"So Parker didn't foot the bill?"

"I think he made a contribution. There were half a dozen others. When they put it all together they didn't have enough for the first roll of the dice. Then, a couple of days later, Parker came back to me, looking bewildered but happy. An anonymous contributor had anted up a hundred grand, with a promise that there was more where that came from if it was needed. Neither Parker nor anyone else on the committee had the faintest idea who Mr. Anonymous was. Sharon Dain couldn't guess who was willing to underwrite her defense. But whoever it was, he's lived up to his word. He came up with another hundred grand before we were done."

"Two hundred grand to defend an obviously guilty woman?" Hardy broke in.

"That's Lieutenant Hardy, Mr. Steiner," Chambrun said.

"You used the right words, Lieutenant. 'Obviously guilty.'" Steiner said. "The police had an open-and-shut case. She lived with Carpenter. She was in the cabin with him that night. There were no fingerprints but hers and his. There are watchmen on the property and none of them saw anyone go into the cabin. It was no secret that Carpenter enjoyed beating her up. She had a motive. But —" and I could hear Steiner let out a long breath—"she swore to me she didn't kill him and I believed her."

"But she pleaded guilty!" Hardy said.

"In self-defense, by reason of insanity," Steiner said. "The curlicues of the law, Lieutenant. I thought I could get her off that way. I knew, with the case the police had, I could never get her off if she pleaded innocent. I tried to get the trial moved away from High Crest. There was too much local sentiment for Carpenter. The court turned me down. The judge who presided was obviously prejudiced. I based the appeals on dozens of exceptions I took to his rulings. The State Supreme Court wouldn't buy. The sentence was improperly heavy, even the way we pleaded. The little lady got just about the worst deal I've ever encountered."

Chambrun cut in. "If she didn't do it she was in the cabin when it was done," he said.

"He had beaten her unconscious that night," Steiner said. "Part of his sexual pleasure, it would seem. When she came to she found him dead, strangled with picture wire."

"She says."

"I believed her," Steiner said. "But there was no way in God's world to make that High Crest jury believe her. I handled it the best and only way I could think of. I was wrong, because it didn't work. But I know damn well if she'd pleaded innocent, she'd have gotten life. As it is she can be out in another ten years."

Chambrun leaned forward. "Has it occurred to you, Mr. Steiner, that, now that some psycho is knocking off people who didn't help Sharon Dain, you might be on his list? You failed her."

Steiner chuckled. "First thing I thought of when I heard the news about an hour ago," he said. "I promise not to turn my back on anyone, not even God. And don't hesitate if I can be of any further help, Mr. Chambrun. I think I'm more anxious than you are to see whoever it is behind bars."

And so, if Steiner was right, Nora's "cheap, rather gaudy little tramp" was rotting away in a women's detention center in Colorado, while the real murderer of Harold Carpenter was walking around free, and some friend of the girl's had set out to knock off anyone who failed to help her. Why had this loony waited so long? The trial that had resulted in Sharon Dain's conviction had been two years ago, but the final appeal had been rejected only a month ago. Our not-so-random killer was just getting warmed up. By an unfortunate chance for us, Chambrun and the hotel, three people who might be on his list were under our roof when he started moving: Hammond, Joanna Fraser, and the man Alvin Parker, of the Parker Foundation, who had been chairman of the defense committee that had failed to save Sharon Dain.

Alvin Parker was, I guessed, in his middle forties. He was prematurely bald, with a sandy-haired fringe around his head, neatly trimmed. He was neatly dressed in a conservative vested suit. His custom-made shoes were neatly polished. I keep repeating the word *neat* because it was the right one for Alvin Parker. He was a neat man.

He seemed surprised to see other people in the office beside Chambrun. He had small grey eyes, which darted from one to the other of us like a doubtful bird's.

"I've been trying to get through to you for the last hour, Mr. Chambrun," he said. "The switchboard wouldn't put me through. And then Miss Ruysdale sent for me." His voice was pleasant, his articulation was—well, neat. I had the feeling that he was just slightly on the comic side, attempting to create an image of superconservative respectability that didn't quite come off.

"I think you must know that we have problems on our hands, Mr. Parker," Chambrun said.

"A ghastly business, from what I've heard," Parker said. "But that's why I had to see you."

"You know something about it?" Chambrun asked.

"Lord, no. But I've been swamped with phone calls, Mr. Chambrun. The Parker Foundation party in the ballroom tonight. People want to know if it's safe to come. Will there be any kind of special protection? Two murders in one day! It's fantastic and it's frightening. It would be a disaster for us if we had to call off the evening."

"I see no reason why the evening should be cancelled," Chambrun said. "There will be protection, and people in groups would appear to be perfectly safe. But I should

72

think what's happened would be particularly shocking to you."

"I don't think I understand," Parker said.

"How did you get the news of our trouble here?"

"Why—why just the announcement you sent around that two people had been murdered in the hotel."

"So you didn't hear on radio or television how the murders were committed?"

"I don't think so," Parker said. "How were they?"

"The two victims were strangled from behind with picture wires," Chambrun said quietly.

"How awful." Then the little bird's eyes widened. "Oh, my God!" he said.

"Quite so," Chambrun said. "The Sharon Dain case. I have to tell you that Geoffrey Hammond and Joanna Fraser were both persons who had refused to help Sharon Dain. I am, you can understand, concerned about anyone who was connected with the Dain case. We are dealing with some kind of psycho who may not only be determined to eliminate anyone who refused to help Sharon Dain but may also have his eye on people who helped and failed. You were chairman of a defense committee set up to help the Dain girl. That committee failed her."

Parker reached out for the back of a chair to steady himself. "You've known this all day and you didn't tell me?" he asked. An unexpected steel crept into his voice.

"I've known it for about ten minutes," Chambrun said, "after I got through talking on the phone to Max Steiner. That's why I sent for you."

"Do you mind if I sit down?" The request was really directed to Nora Coyle, who was standing over by the sideboard. The perfect little gentleman, our Alvin. He shook his head. "I did everything I could for that girl. Why someone should have it in for me because it wasn't enough—?" He looked around at all of us for answers.

"There's not much point in trying to make it make sense," Chambrun said. "The young man who went

73

around this city shooting young couples in parked cars, you remember? There were all kinds of speculations, before he was caught, as to what his motives could be. When he was caught he gave a reason no one had dreamed of. Demons, he said, had ordered him to kill."

"We are looking for some kind of psycho, Mr. Parker," Hardy said. "So far the two people he has killed—killed the same way Harold Carpenter was killed—were people who refused to help Sharon Dain. Right now, any kind of connection with the Dain case puts you on the danger list."

"But there were so many—" Parker said.

"Start with the defense committee," Hardy suggested.

"I—I'd have to go back to my diaries," Parker said. "There was a young movie star, Lance Wilson; and Sheila Wallace, the Hollywood columnist; and Dave Trumbell, the Olympic skiing coach. Others. I'll have to check for you."

"The person we're looking for is here, not out there," Hardy said. "Do you think if you went through the Beaumont's list of registered guests you might recognize names of people who had some remote connection with the case, who may have been at High Crest at the time of the murder?"

"That must include hundreds of names," Parker said.

"Hundreds of names, approximately a thousand people with more than one person registered to a room or suite," Chambrun said.

Parker glanced at his watch. "I could do it, of course," he said. "But there is so little time before the fund-raising ball tonight and so much to be done. Tomorrow?"

"It may be your hide that's at stake," Hardy said sharply.

"Yes. Of course. I must then, mustn't I?"

"Get him the list, Ruysdale," Chambrun said, and Miss Ruysdale moved swiftly out to her own office. "There are two things that interest me, Mr. Parker," Chambrun went

74

on. "The first may seem irrelevant to you. Your presence at High Crest in the skiing season; forgive me if I say you don't strike me as the athletic type, a skiing enthusiast."

Parker gave him a rueful little smile. "You're quite right, Mr. Chambrun, I'm not. My interest in High Crest is a financial one."

"You have money in it?"

"Oh, no, not personally. My late uncle, Joshua Parker, put up the money to build High Crest into what it is. The profits, in which his estate shares, go to the Parker Foundation, of which I am president and executive director. It is routine for me to go to High Crest in the height of their season to see how things are going and to make sure the foundation isn't being ripped off by the High Crest management. My job is to keep them honest."

"So you knew Harold Carpenter? He'd been on the staff there for some years."

"Yes, I knew him." Parker's face clouded.

"And didn't like him?"

Parker spread his hands in a little gesture of helplessness. "You are a man who manages a place that deals with people, Mr. Chambrun. Your guests, your staff. You don't like them all, I'm sure. Carpenter was expert at what he did, which was to teach skiing. One of the best. As a human being, I thought him impossibly arrogant. But I must confess that I don't like noisy extroverts. He was an important cog in the machine to the management at High Crest. He was an attraction they sold to the public. I didn't interfere with their hiring and firing, only in an accounting of their profits."

"You knew Sharon Dain?" Chambrun asked.

"I met her on that visit two years ago," Parker said.

"And your opinion of her?"

Parker hesitated. You could tell he was a man who didn't express opinions without giving them careful thought. "For my tastes she was not attractive," Parker said. "Rather coarse, rather vulgar. But physically? I don't think any man could look at her and not be, shall I say, slightly stirred." He glanced at Nora. "Sexy is the word, I guess."

"And you chose to help defend her."

"I chose to believe her story," Parker said.

"Which story?"

"I don't understand," Parker said.

"Steiner tells us that she first claimed to be innocent. That she hadn't killed Carpenter. That she was unconscious when it happened. Later she pleaded guilty, claiming self-defense and legal insanity."

"I believe she didn't kill Carpenter," Parker said slowly, very precisely. "It was Steiner who pointed out that with the case the police had she didn't stand a chance with a plea of innocent. He thought he could get her off the other way. He failed." Parker's eyes widened. "Could he be a target for this—this psycho you're looking for?"

"He could be," Chambrun said. "You hired him, didn't you, Mr. Parker?"

"Technically, yes. I made the contact, but it was the consensus of the defense committee. Only the best."

"But you didn't have the funds to meet his fee?"

"I'm not a rich man, Mr. Chambrun, but I put up five thousand dollars. Lance Wilson did the same, and a couple of others. But we weren't even at square one. Then, out of the blue, came this handsome contribution—a hundred thousand—from someone we've never been able to identify. It was duplicated later. Amazing!"

"No clue at all?"

"None."

"How was the money delivered?"

"In cash, in a box, delivered by United Parcel. If the driver had known what he was delivering he'd probably have fainted. The sender's name was Dain, the address a hotel in Denver."

"A relative of Sharon Dain's?"

"She swears she has no relatives, no family. As a matter

76

of fact, 'Sharon Dain' is a stage name, not her real name. Her real name is, I believe, Elizabeth Schwartz. We figured the donor simply used the Dain name as a cover."

"Sharon Dain was an actress?"

Parker shrugged. "Small bits, an extra in films. I guess she hadn't found the right casting couches."

"Carpenter's couch wasn't exactly ideal," Chambrun said.

Parker shook his head. "I'm told that some people enjoy violence in connection with sex," he said. "Carpenter was evidently too much of a good thing. Whips and chains."

"How's that?" Chambrun asked.

"I'm told some people use whips and chains and other instruments of torture in their sexual orgies." The small birdlike eyes were very bright.

Chambrun leaned back in his chair. I wondered if he was thinking what I was, that our neat little man could be moved by the thought of offbeat sex.

"Now, if you will go through our list of registered guests, Mr. Parker," Chambrun said.

Parker glanced at his wristwatch. "Four o'clock," he said. "There is so much to do before tonight. But I'll do my best."

We watched him go out to Ruysdale's office where she had the list prepared for him.

"God knows what they do at a ski resort in the summertime," Chambrun said, "but how would you like to take a trip to Colorado, Mark?"

I just stared at him.

"The police out there will cooperate," Hardy said.

"If the police out there got the wrong person for the murder of Harold Carpenter, they aren't going to cooperate with anyone who's looking for the right one," Chambrun said, "and that right one may be here in the Beaumont getting ready to hit someone else."

"But I'm not a detective!" I protested.

"People involved will talk a lot more freely to someone

77

unofficial," Chambrun said. "Go pack. Hardy and I will draw up a plan of action for you."

CHAPTER TWO

When Chambrun plans and organizes something you can count on its being thorough.

Nora Coyle and I went down the hall to my apartment, she, ostensibly, to get her things and find another place. I persuaded her she could stay there.

"There's booze, coffee, some odds and ends in the frig," I told her. "A hi-fi system, records, books. Best place in the hotel."

"But you don't want a stranger—"

"I dream of your being a lot less of a stranger one of these days," I said. "You'll be just down the hall from where the action is."

That was an understatement. I'd just gotten a bag out of my closet and was looking in my shirt drawer when the phone rang. It was Ruysdale.

"Your plane leaves for Colorado from Kennedy," she said. "You have less than an hour and a half to pack, pick up your instructions here, and get out there."

They must have been burning up the long-distance wires in Chambrun's office. When I got there, after giving Nora a good-bye brotherly kiss on the cheek, they had information and plans for me.

Hardy had arranged for me to interview Sharon Dain at the prison where she was held. Nine o'clock tomorrow morning.

"Get some sleep on the plane," Chambrun said. "You get out there at ten-forty, mountain time. You will be met by Mike Chandler, manager of High Crest, courtesy of

Alvin Parker. There are two people Steiner suggests you see. One is a private eye who worked for him, name of Jack Galt. Don't bother to make notes, Mark. It's all on this paper I've prepared for you."

"I'm already numb," I said.

"In addition to Galt, there is a reporter for the local press, female, Sandy Potter. Sandra, I suspect. It seems she never believed in Sharon Dain's guilt. She knows people. She covers High Crest in season. After you've talked to these people you play it by ear."

"Right now I'm stone deaf," I said.

Chambrun gave me his patient-parent look. "Mark, we are looking for someone else beside Sharon Dain who may have killed Carpenter. Carpenter was strangled with picture wire, and two people here have been hit the same way. It can't be Sharon Dain who is at work here. So it is not improbable that it's the same person, same method. So who is he, and what was his motive for killing Carpenter in the first place? Still deaf?"

"There's still a whirring noise," I said. "If Galt and this girl reporter couldn't find that answer two years ago, how do you expect me, following a cold trail—"

"Because now we know more than they did," Chambrun said.

"We do?"

"Snap out of it, Mark," Chambrun said, no longer patient. "Two years ago they played with the idea that Sharon Dain was innocent. Steiner believed she was, Galt and the girl reporter worked on that premise. Someone had it in for Carpenter, got into the cabin where Sharon Dain was unconscious from a beating. Like here, it was someone Carpenter didn't fear. He turned his back and got strangled. Motive? Two years ago it could have been a hundred different things. They didn't have an idea who it was, so they couldn't begin to guess who had it in for Carpenter or why. Now we can make a good guess."

"I'm glad you can," I said. "I don't see—"

"There's no time to suggest that you *think,*" Chambrun said. "The killer cared for Sharon Dain, had his eye on her at least, and killed Carpenter for the way he treated her. He waits for the trial and all the appeals to be over and then, still caring for the girl, he sets out to knock off people who failed her. The same motive, the same psychotic driving force, could fit all three cases. So you're looking for some boyfriend out of Sharon Dain's past, or someone who was trying to take her away from Carpenter two years ago. Sharon Dain may tell you, she may not. I have a hunch you're looking for a very rich man. Could be a movie star, someone she knew in Hollywood."

"You think the murderer may be the mysterious person who put up the money for Steiner's fee?" I asked.

"Good boy," Chambrun said. "I was beginning to be concerned about you."

I have never enjoyed flying. If something goes wrong with a car you're driving you can get out and walk. It's childish, but I don't feel comfortable in the air. There was to be a stopover in Chicago, and then on to Denver. High Crest, I'd been told, was about thirty miles from the airport there.

Chambrun's last word to me was a suggestion that I shouldn't try to invent answers till I had some facts. I was to sleep. That was an order! One I couldn't obey.

I had a couple of drinks on the way to Chicago, a couple in the airport there, and a couple more on the way to Denver. I was feeling no pain when I got off the plane at Denver and looked around for someone who might be there to meet me. The airport clocks said a quarter to eleven, but it was a quarter to one my time and I was ready to hit the sack anywhere.

A tall, lean man wearing blue jeans, cowboy boots, Stetson, and a gaudy shirt walked up to me. He had a neatly trimmed red beard and pleasant blue eyes with a mass of crow's-feet at their corners.

"Mr. Haskell?" he asked. "I'm Mike Chandler, the manager at High Crest."

"How did you spot me?"

He grinned. "You looked lost," he said. "Let me take your bag."

He led me out into a parking lot and to, of all things, a Rolls-Royce station wagon.

"Take us about thirty minutes," he said as we pulled out of the lot.

I didn't say anything for a few minutes, and then I said, "With you driving."

He grinned, without looking at me. "Too fast for you? We learn to cover distances in a hurry out here."

"I left my parachute in the plane," I said.

He laughed, but he didn't ease up any.

"I take it this is a slow season for you," I said, to make conversation.

"Hell, no," he said. "We turn to dude ranching in the summertime. Horses, trail riding, camping trips. We're bursting at the seams with customers. I wouldn't have had a place for you if Alvin Parker hadn't insisted."

I was suddenly conscious of the air. We don't get to breath anything like it in my part of the world. Chandler took a corner like you wouldn't believe. We were climbing. It was a beautiful night, full moon, a million stars. On a straightaway Chandler gave me a sidelong glance.

"I'm not sure I'm exactly happy about your being here, Mr. Haskell," he said.

"Opening up old wounds?"

"It's not good for business," he said.

"Don't worry," I said. "I've got some people to talk to. Your guests won't know I'm alive. Of course, you're one of the people I need to talk to. Do you know why it's opened up again?"

"Mr. Parker told me. It's crazy, you know."

"I know. Which side were you on two years ago?"

"Side?"

81

"The prosecution or the defense?"

"Man, you're involved with running a hotel, I understand," Chandler said. "You know you don't take sides. The customer is always right. 'Yes, sir! You're absolutely right!' And just the reverse to the next one."

"But which side were you really on?" I persisted.

He seemed to push down on the gas pedal. We were doing eighty, going uphill and around curves. Indianapolis lost a great competitor in this cowboy.

"There are things that sometimes make you feel two ways," he said. He fished a cigarette out of his shirt pocket. I wished he'd keep both hands on the wheel. I held my lighter for him. He laughed. "Fingertip control," he said. And the sonofabitch took everything off the wheel but one finger. Then he stopped playing games and went back to my question. "Hal Carpenter was not my favorite man," he said. "He made trouble for me, but he also attracted special customers I couldn't afford to lose. He was brilliant on skis, and just as brilliant as a teacher. Lot of the big male stars in Hollywood came here on account of him and what he could teach them about the sport. Those were the customers I couldn't afford to lose. They came, and they sent their friends—because of Hal. Women? That was another story."

"Oh?"

"He attracted them, like a moth to a night-light. There was talk about his technique. He liked to play rough. Some women enjoy that. Some of them ran away screaming after a taste of it. It was those who gave me trouble." Chandler was suddenly gripping the wheel as if he was driving a truck, his mouth a thin, straight line under the red beard.

"So when it happened you figured he'd got what was coming to him?"

Chandler nodded. "And that spelled woman to me," he said. "The picture-wire deal was the way a woman might have gone about it, I thought. Carpenter could have taken

82

on Muhammad Ali in his prime and done pretty well. He wouldn't have let an angry man get behind him. So, Sharon Dain was there with him, he'd been beating the hell out of her for a couple of weeks. She may have liked it at first. Maybe she still liked it, and he was about to give her the gate. But it had to be her."

"The cops had no doubts."

"None. Neither did I. *Do* I. But—well, I gave a hundred bucks to Mr. Parker's defense committee."

"To stay on his good side?"

"Not exactly. I felt Sharon had been driven to it and was entitled to help." Chandler's laugh was mirthless. "She'd solved a problem for me. I was just about at the end of my rope with Carpenter."

"What is she like—Sharon Dain?"

We had reached a high spot on the winding road we were traveling. Below us was a deep valley, silver in the moonlight. Across the valley, at about the same height we were at on this side, were what looked like a thousand lights.

Chandler gestured. "High Crest," he said.

"Looks like a city!" I said.

"Small town," he said.

It was going to be like a roller-coaster ride, down into the valley and then up again. My stomach did a roller-coaster flip-flop as we started down. Chandler seemed to increase speed rather than reducing it.

"Women, women, women," he said.

Glancing at him I thought he probably did all right with the girls himself. He was lean, hard, dashing in a kind of way. He must be constantly surrounded by them at his High Crest resort. I wondered if Harold Carpenter had been a kind of rival.

"I see 'em in all shapes and sizes and stations of life at High Crest," he said. The tires on the Rolls screeched a little as we took a hairpin right, headed down. "They have to have money, or their men have to have money, if they come to High Crest. But they're a special breed. They've either made it big themselves, probably in films, or they've made men who've made it. It isn't high society, like you have back in, say, Newport. They're mostly at High Crest because they're good in somebody's bed. Most of them are ornaments to some male ego."

"Strange place for Joanna Fraser to have held a convention of women libbers," I said.

Chandler laughed. "Those gals created quite a problem," he said. "They came without men, and they damn near created a riot going after the men who were there and already had women with them. They talked a great ball game about not being 'sex objects,' but they sure had an appetite for it after they got through telling you their slogans."

"Sharon Dain?" I suggested again.

"Carpenter came to me that January," Chandler said, "and told me he was bringing his own woman to High Crest for a while. We've got maybe a hundred cabins scattered around the main complex of buildings, and Carpenter had the use of one of them in the skiing season. This woman he was bringing would stay there with him. I didn't object. Most of the cabins are occupied by people who haven't been sanctified by the Pope. Nobody bothers these days to sign 'Mr. and Mrs.' People living together, not married, is the name of the game. They even have children, not married, and the gossip columnists write about it and nobody cares. Not like when I was a kid and you took a girl to a hotel, signed 'Mr. and Mrs.,' and tried not to look at the room clerk so you wouldn't see his cynical smile. No, I didn't object to Carpenter's having a woman in his cabin. It might keep him from making passes at other women who belonged to other men."

"So Sharon Dain was the woman Carpenter brought to his cabin," I said. I wondered if Chandler just wandered in his conversation by habit, or if he was deliberately avoiding the subject of Sharon Dain.

We were racing across the floor of the valley, with High Crest almost directly above us, looking like something perched on top of a skyscraper.

"Yeah, she was the one," Chandler said. "She wasn't usual. I mean, a lot of the women who come to High Crest in the skiing season don't ski. But they dress for it. Pants, turtlenecks, wool toques, boots. Expensive, you understand, but winter sports. Sharon didn't even pretend she was there for the skiing. Most of the time she looked like an actress who had been dressed by a costume designer for some porno movie. One zip of her zipper and she'd be ready for action. I suspect that look had gotten her wherever she was in films, which wasn't very far. A man couldn't look at her and think about the weather, or the skiing surface, or the downhill slope. All you could think about was taking her someplace and letting her demonstrate what she was obviously good at."

"Pretty?" I asked.

"In an artificial way. False eyelashes, makeup. But built like you wouldn't believe."

"So, did she solve your problems with Carpenter?"

"Not really. He was a guy who was designed to preside over a harem. My wife called him 'the golden gooser.' "

I hadn't heard about a wife before. We were charging up a mountain at what seemed to me a reckless speed.

"Back in New York they're wondering if Sharon had some other boyfriend, maybe from her past, who resented Carpenter and decided to do him in," I said.

"She probably had dozens of them," Chandler said, tight-lipped again. "Boyfriends were her stock in trade. But there was no one here that January I could point a finger at. Oh, there are men who come here with a woman one season, and a different one the next season. And the first woman is here with some other dude. Everyone acts like strangers. Sharon had never been here before, so there was no way I could tell if there was someone here then who'd been involved with her past. Could have been, but I had no way of knowing." He took a corner so fast I shut my eyes. "Sharon was attractive, alluring even, but you could tell she came from way over on the wrong side of the tracks."

There were lights everywhere, in the windows of the buildings, outside the front doors, hanging from poles in a sort of compound surrounded by cottages, in a huge main building, and in little shops where they apparently sold western clothes, boots, tack for western riders. I imagined all these were turned into ski shops in the wintertime.

"How many people can you take care of here?" I asked Chandler, as he pulled up outside the main building.

He leaned back, flexing his fingers. Maybe he wasn't as relaxed as he looked, driving that crazy way. "People doubled up, and mostly they do," he said, "about three hundred and fifty. Cabins will take more than two if someone doesn't mind sleeping on the couch. When there's a ski jump in the winter season, we have squeezed in over four hundred."

Windows to the main house were open on this cool June night and I could hear a low murmur of voices and laughter against a background of someone giving a very good imitation of the late Fats Waller on a piano. "Ain't misbehavin'—I'm savin' my love for you."

"Party?" I asked.

"Every night," he said. "Just sitting around. Freddy Lukes can keep 'em occupied as long as we want to sell booze."

"Lukes?"

"Black piano player," Chandler said.

He carried my bag into a huge, high-ceilinged room, dimly lit. There were two enormous fireplaces at either end of the room with low fires burning, for cheer not heat. Couples were draped around on couches, on the floor. There was a bar at one side of the room, handled by two white-coated bartenders. Opposite, on a little raised platform, was an upright piano. The black man playing was lighted by a little pinspot over his head. He wore black glasses even in the semidarkness. He broke into "Honeysuckle Rose," one of Fats Waller's best, as we came in.

"I've got a room for you in the main building," Chandler said, "if you can sleep over the noise. They'll keep at it till probably around one or two o'clock."

That reminded me of the time difference. They had a couple of hours to go.

"I could sleep in a boiler factory," I said. "A little jet lag, I guess. I've an appointment at Sharon Dain's jail at nine in the morning."

"I'll have you called at seven," Chandler said. "The state prison is about an hour away. I'll provide a car for you."

"With you driving that's about a hundred miles," I said.

He laughed. "Not me. It's about forty-five miles."

Everybody in the room was dressed like cowboys and cowgirls. A blond cowgirl came over from the bar to join us.

"Welcome, Mr. Haskell," she said.

"My wife, Nikki," Chandler said. I found out the spelling later.

Nikki Chandler had a curious charm of her own. Late thirties, I thought, tanned mahogany brown from the sun. Hair worn shoulder length, bleached by that same sun. Endless exposure to weather, summer and winter I supposed, gave her skin a leathery look, fine little wrinkles at the corners of her blue eyes and across her high forehead. She was slim, athletic looking, with not too much in the way of bosoms. But there was a kind of tension about her, very near the surface, as if she was waiting for someone to provide her with an excruciating excitement. The way she looked at me I had to believe she was wondering if I might be that someone. It was flattering.

"I've been trying to remember when I got off the jet

and into Mike's Rolls," I said to her. "Both experiences were about the same."

She glanced at her man. "Did you ask him to slow down, Mr. Haskell?"

"Against my better judgment, no."

"You get a drink on the house for that," she said. "Mike's main pleasure in life is to scare people out of their wits, force them to ask him to let up on the pedal." Then to Mike, "Lance Wilson asked to see you as soon as you got back."

"Lance Wilson is here? What luck," I said. That, I thought, would save me a trip to Hollywood.

"Have someone show Mr. Haskell his room," Mike said.

"My pleasure," Nikki said.

Mike Chandler handed me my bag and Nikki led me across the room to a rear exit. No one seemed to be interested in a newcomer, even though I looked out of place in my tan slacks, navy sports shirt, and seersucker jacket among all those fake cowpokes.

Nikki took me down a long hallway off which dozens of rooms seemed to open. The one for me was at the very end of the line. It was a small room with two built-in bunks, one above the other, with a little ladder to the upper berth. Off it was a tiny bathroom—basin, stall shower, john. You'd be apt to bump your elbows shaving.

"I promised you a free drink," Nikki said. "What'll it be? I can have it sent to you or you can join me at the bar."

"A double Jack Daniels on the rocks ought to put me to sleep," I said. "And of course you don't have to buy it."

She stood in the middle of the tiny room, not making any move to leave. "I remember staying at the Beaumont, your hotel, Mark, long ago. They presented me with a split of champagne and fresh flowers when I checked in. We're not quite that fancy, but a double Jack Daniels is easy. Here or out there?"

"Having a drink with you is something I'd better regret having to delay," I said. "I've got to be up at the crack of dawn, my time, to get over to the state prison. May I have a rain check?"

She didn't move. I've been looked over by women before, and I have to confess I felt a kind of weary excitement at the way she was studying me. Any other time, I thought.

"It's not going to be exactly fun to go over old history," she said. "Why do you have to?"

"You know what's happened in New York, at the Beaumont?"

She nodded. "It was on the tube," she said.

"The three cases have to be tied together somehow," I said. "We're trying to stop a killer before he strikes again."

"But you won't find him here," she said. "He's obviously in New York."

"A lead to him," I said.

"Sharon Dain's in jail, convicted of the crime that happened here," she said.

"There are people who don't believe she did it, including her lawyer," I said.

She kept giving me that calculating look. I began to think, reluctantly, that it wasn't sex that interested her. "Certainly Sharon Dain wasn't in the Beaumont early this morning," she said. She gave me a wry little smile. "The only person at High Crest who could have been there then is you."

"But I wasn't here two years ago," I said. "If Sharon Dain isn't guilty, why do you resent my looking into it?"

"I don't resent it for that reason," she said. "But it's hopeless, Mark. Steiner is the best, but he failed. A very good private eye named Jack Galt tried, and he failed. Sandra Potter, a first-class newspaper woman, also tried, and she failed. It's dead end out here, Mark."

"Maybe they didn't ask the right questions or talk to the right people," I said. I remembered Chambrun's line. "We know more now than anyone did back then."

"Hal Carpenter got what was coming to him," she said,

89

and her voice was suddenly not quite steady.

"But someone has now gone off his rocker and is killing people who had almost no connection with the early case. He's got to be stopped, and he has to have some connection with what happened out here."

She was suddenly a statue there in the center of my room, staring past me at something she wanted to forget.

"Mike and I contributed to the Sharon Dain defense fund," she said.

"I know. He told me."

"But he didn't tell you why."

"I made a guess," I said. "To stay on the right side of Alvin Parker. Mike said it wasn't that."

"It wasn't that."

To my surprise her whole tense body seemed to be shaking. I waited for her to go on.

"One night, long ago, I stopped at Hal Carpenter's cabin to deliver a message about some lesson cancellation for the next day," she said. "There are no phones in the cabins. He suggested I come in for a drink. I knew his reputation but I thought I was too old to interest him, and besides that, I was the boss's wife." A nerve twitched high up on her cheek. "He closed the door when I came in, turned, ripped off my clothes—being a man you've never been raped, Mark."

"My God!" I said. "And he was kept on here after that?"

"I didn't tell Mike—then," she said. "He would have tried to kill Hal, and Hal was too tough for him. I didn't tell him till after Hal was dead. Mike was all for having Sharon Dain burned at the stake. I felt, whatever she'd done, she deserved help after polishing off that animal! I would have done it myself if I'd had the guts!"

"But you wouldn't have gone on doing it," I said. "Someone has. Someone who first tried to save Sharon Dain from taking the rap for a crime he'd committed by paying for her defense; someone who has waited for all the appeals to fail before starting to punish the people

90

who wouldn't help. Then, maybe there'll be a third category. People who didn't help enough! It can go on and on, Nikki."

"What I just told you—and a lot of other garbage that could destroy High Crest—can come out if the case here is reopened," Nikki said.

"And other people can get killed if this psycho isn't stopped," I said. I reached out and touched her hand. It was like ice. "Some bright boy in the press is going to remind people of two years ago when the connection is made, and it can't miss being made. I was sent out here to avoid the sensation a police investigation would cause —and because we don't trust the local police to admit they could have been wrong about Sharon Dain. I have one question to ask anyone I talk to. What other men were interested in Sharon Dain two years ago, or before that?"

Nikki was still the frozen statue, not looking directly at me any more. The past was torturing her—a sophisticated woman brutally mauled by a punk. I wondered what it had done to her relationship with Mike Chandler. She couldn't forget, and I suspected he couldn't forget.

"No man," she said in a low voice, "who had any contact with Sharon Dain could miss knowing that she was ready, any time, any place. You keep hunting, Mark, and you'll find a list as long as your arm. I can't name anyone in particular. The time she was here she was strictly Hal Carpenter's property. No one at High Crest at that time was going to make a play for her. Hal was too dangerous to mix with, and he showed her off as belonging to him quite openly. I don't think anyone killed him because he got in the way of a dream. So if you're right, it must have been someone out of her past, before she ever came here."

"But who was a guest at High Crest at that time," I said. "You must have a list of who was staying here at the time of Carpenter's murder."

"Of course," she said almost impatiently. "The police

91

have it, too, and they came up with nothing."

"They weren't looking," I said. "They had Sharon Dain trussed up like a Christmas turkey. Can I see that list?"

She took a breath and let it out in a long sigh. "I suppose there's no reason why not. In the morning?"

"Fine," I said. "If I could have it before I take off to see Sharon Dain, I could look at it on the way. It might make me smarter in talking to her. And take it easy, Nikki. What you told me doesn't have to go public."

"Thanks," she said. She moved. "A double Jack Daniels, you said? I'll have one of the barboys bring it down."

CHAPTER THREE

I was almost gone before the barboy came with my drink, and I was out like a light a few moments after I'd had it. The fresh mountain air drifting through my screened window was like a drug.

Someone was pounding on my door in what seemed like five minutes later. I mumbled something and opened my eyes. It was daylight outside.

"Mike Chandler here, Mark," the knocker said. "Seven o'clock. Breakfast in fifteen minutes."

I thanked him and struggled out of bed. A shave and shower seemed to bring me back to life. The damned time change made it nine o'clock on my schedule. I'd had about six hours sleep. My bloodshot eyes looked it. I put on a pair of tinted glasses I use for driving and went down the hall to find breakfast.

There was a dining room off the big hall I'd seen last night. Quite a few cowboys and cowgirls were already up and eating. Mike Chandler was waiting for me at the entrance and took me to a table, set up for four.

"All-day trail ride," he said, indicating the people. "We start early. What'll it be, eggs, bacon, ham, corned beef hash? There may even be some brook trout."

"Juice, a couple of boiled eggs, toast and coffee would be fine," I said. "If I could have the coffee now—"

I realized then that the breakfast was served buffet style, self-service, but Chandler was going to take care of me. He brought me coffee and went back to the buffet. I was feeling grateful for the first swallow when I was joined by a young man I recognized without ever having seen him in the flesh before. He was Lance Wilson, the movie actor.

"Mark has told me why you're here, Haskell," he said. He didn't bother to mention his name. Everyone was expected to know that on sight. "Mind if I sit down?"

"Help yourself."

I don't quite know how to describe Lance Wilson. He could have been trying to look like Robert Redford, or trying not to look like him and not able to make it. Being too like a famous star is bad for a career. There were never two Clark Gables, or two Gary Coopers, or two Jimmy Cagneys. Lance Wilson was the clean-cut-Robert-Redford-American-boy. In his cowboy clothes he looked like the Sundance Kid.

He sat down. He'd brought coffee with him. He offered me a cigarette, which I refused, and lit one for himself. I have to have that first cup of coffee before I start killing myself with nicotine.

"A lot of us had hoped that two years ago was gone and forgotten," he said.

"I can imagine," I said.

"It's not good in my business to get yourself connected with a crime or a scandal," he said. "The big wheels get awfully moral when they're not involved themselves. I've only just started to get some decent jobs again."

"But how were you involved?" I asked.

"Gave my name to the Sharon Dain Defense Commit-

93

tee," he said. "Not a sensible thing to do, it seems."

"But nice, and human," I said.

He inhaled on his cigarette. "I've learned it's better not to show your human side in this business. It cost me."

I looked across the rim of my coffee cup at him. "You had some connection with Sharon Dain?"

"God, no," he said. "That is, not till she was in trouble. Never laid eyes on her till I saw her here with Carpenter that January. But—well, I was willing to help anyone get off the hook who had trouble with him. You remember the movie *Jaws*?"

"Who doesn't?"

"I was supposed to have one of the leads in that but I couldn't make it." His eyes were steel cold. "Carpenter tried to mess around with a girl I brought up here. I called him for it. He beat the shit out of me out on the slope one afternoon. I couldn't go in front of the camera for six weeks. Lost a big chance." He shrugged. "So when I heard someone polished off the miserable bastard I was willing to help the little lady take as small a beating as possible."

"Help generously, I hear."

"Five grand," he said. "Alvin Parker and I were the big sugar daddies on the committee, but when we counted it all up Max Steiner just laughed at us. Then Sharon's fairy godmother waved her wand and up came support from Mr. or Ms. Anonymous."

"No clue as to who that was?"

He gave me a very direct, sincere, Robert Redford look. "You notice I said *'Mr. or Ms.'*—Miz, that is. Been thinking about it ever since I heard you'd come out here to smell around; after I heard what happened in the Beaumont in New York."

"You think a woman may have made the big donation?" I asked.

"We were inundated with unattached women that January," Wilson said. "Liberation convention. They supported all women's causes, including homes for unwed

94

mothers. Is it unreasonable to think that Sharon Dain may have seemed like a worthy cause to some of them?"

"Joanna Frazer turned her down," I said. "The thinking in New York is that that's why this crazy killer went after her."

"Maybe all he knew about was the turndown," Wilson said. "Joanna Fraser had the kind of bread Anonymous put up. She may not have wanted to support a murderess publicly, but privately it could have been her kind of cause. Maybe it's too bad for her she kept it a secret."

It certainly wasn't a notion that had occurred to me before. I wondered if Nora Coyle had been holding out on me, and if so, why? It didn't change my goal, though. I told Wilson we were looking for some man in Sharon Dain's past who was getting revenge for what had been done to her.

"I can't help you there," he said. "I never heard of the girl until that New Year's week out here. But Max Steiner hired a supposedly very competent private investigator named Galt who, I understand, did an in-depth study of her past, looking for anything that would help."

Mike Chandler was at my elbow, putting down my juice, eggs, and toast in front of me.

"Galt's on his way from Hollywood to see you, Mark," he said. "He phoned last night after you'd turned in. Max Steiner asked him to cooperate with you. He should be here by the time you get back from seeing Sharon at the prison."

The eggs were just to my liking. I kept looking around for Nikki, who had promised me the guest list from two years back to take on my trip. Mike Chandler had joined us at the table with his coffee.

"Your wife doesn't get up with these early birds?" I asked.

"Nikki? First one up. She's overseeing the lunch we take on our trail ride." Mike laughed. "Caviar among the mountain goats. We take the comforts of life very seriously at High Crest." Then he patted at the pocket of his fancy shirt. "I almost forgot," he said. "She gave me something for you."

It was the list I wanted.

I had gone down in the class of my transportation. It was a four-wheel-drive Scout that would have been left far behind by Mike Chandler's Rolls. My driver was a high school boy about seventeen, who told me this was his first summer job at High Crest. He hadn't been dry behind the ears when Hal Carpenter was murdered and knew nothing about the case except for some unreliable gossip he'd heard around the bunkhouse. After a few minutes of gaping at the unbelievable beauty of the sun-drenched mountains I started to study the list Nikki Chandler had left for me. It was a machine-duplicated copy of the original, which must have gone to the police. It was smeared a little in some places. There must have been three hundred and fifty names on it.

It didn't do me much good. There were, of course, names that connected. Joanna Fraser was there, and Nora Coyle, and Sharon Dain herself, Lance Wilson and maybe a dozen other movie names I recognized, and Sandra Potter, the girl reporter I was supposed to contact, and Alvin Parker. There was one name, Charles Davis from Las Vegas, which had a question mark written after it in pencil. I'd have to ask Nikki what that meant. Some of the gals in the convention group had names in the world of women's lib. I'd actually seen a couple of them around the Beaumont in the past few years. I put check marks after them because they just might be worth a further look. But put them all together and they didn't spell "mother."

My driver wasn't Mike Chandler, but he drove a nice, steady run, and at about twenty minutes to nine the grey stone walls of the prison loomed up ahead of us. I was going to make my appointment on time.

I thought afterward that it was a good thing I had. The

authorities were anything but friendly. I think they'd have used any excuse to turn me around and tell me to go peddle my papers. The prison guard who took me down a long, cold corridor to what I assumed was some kind of interrogation room, probably bugged, looked at me as though he'd caught me driving without a license and with some pot stashed away in my glove compartment.

"How much time do I have?" I asked him, as he ushered me into a small square space with white-washed walls, a small table, and two straight-backed kitchen chairs.

"Half an hour," he said, and slammed the door on me.

I had the uncomfortable feeling that I was locked in and might never get out. I think I was a little stir-crazy within thirty seconds.

It was ten minutes after nine when a woman jailer ushered Sharon Dain into my presence. I wondered if that ten-minute delay counted in my half hour.

None of the things anybody had told me about Sharon Dain was true that morning. This was no sex queen. There were no seductive false eyelashes or makeup; the grey prison clothes disguised what Mike Chandler had described as "built like you wouldn't believe." Dark hair was cut short. Narrowed dark eyes looked at me with a kind of hostility that actually hurt. You sensed how desperately alone she was.

"Who are you and what the hell do you want?" she asked. Her voice was harsh, almost as if she hadn't used it for a long time and had to force it to work.

I told her my name. I told her the New York police had arranged for this interview. Then I realized she had no idea why the New York police could be interested in her, and I told her what had happened at the Beaumont.

"Sweet Jesus!" she said.

I offered her a cigarette and she almost grabbed the whole pack. Her hands were shaking. I held my lighter for her and she dragged smoke down into the bottom of the well. Then she sat down in one of the chairs, rigid.

"One thing is for certain, Haskell," she said. "They don't give you a furlough from this joint. I sure as hell didn't kill anyone in your hotel. What am I supposed to be able to do for you?"

"Maybe I'm the one who can do something for you," I said. "Max Steiner still believes you didn't kill Hal Carpenter. Now, after what's happened in New York, other people are beginning to wonder."

"You mean there's some chance I might—?"

"A chance. A good chance. But we need help."

" 'We'? What's in it for you, Haskell?"

"To keep someone else from getting killed, particularly in the Beaumont."

She turned her head and looked around the upper molding of the white-washed walls. "You know this goddamned room is probably bugged," she said. "You can't go to the john in this cave without someone watching, listening."

"Can't be helped," I said. "Try to listen to me, Sharon, and think while you're listening. In New York they think there's a pattern that goes something like this: A man who loved you, or wanted you so badly he was ready to kill Carpenter for the way he was abusing you. Then you get hooked for it. He doesn't want to turn himself in, naturally, but he doesn't mean for you to be convicted. He puts up the money for your defense."

Her sudden laugh was bitter. "Mr. Anonymous? I tell you something, Haskell. I've been surrounded by men ever since I was fourteen years old. But I never knew one who'd put up two hundred thousand bucks for me."

"Let me finish," I said. "This man waits for your trial to be over; he waits for the appeals, down to the very last one, which was denied a month ago. He can't save you, but he's crazy enough to set out to punish the people who wouldn't help, or perhaps failed you. We don't think he's through."

"He's not doing me any good, whoever he is," she said.

98

"He's got to be stopped, Sharon. Two people already dead, and maybe more to come."

She gave me a look that made me uneasy, as if she was trying to read something very private about me. I had no idea what it might be.

"I don't know how to help you," she said. "When I got out to Hollywood as a teen-age kid, I believed what I'd heard—that the way to a career in the movies was to sleep with the right people. At first what I got were extra players and stage hands, the bottom-of-the-drawer agents and studio executives. Oh, I got one or two screen tests but nobody took any trouble with them. I guess my guys were the go-no-place people in the business. The film business, I mean. Because I suddenly had a business of my own." She gave me a bitter little smile. "I found I had a special talent for listening to men who had big troubles. The little mother of all the world! But someone who would put up almost a quarter of a million bucks to help me out of a jam!" She shook her head slowly from side to side. "Could I have been comforting a gold mine and didn't know it?"

"How did you get involved with Harold Carpenter?" I asked her.

She smiled again, that bitter little smile. "My usual run of good luck," she said. "I was hanging around a bar in L.A., looking for something promising to turn up. This handsome guy comes in, fancy sports clothes, smelling of money, I thought. He slides down the bar to where I am, offers to buy me a drink. The usual pickup." She dropped her cigarette on the floor and stamped it out. "Don't give me the critical eye, Haskell. I'm a professional hooker and I don't care who knows it. It wouldn't matter now, would it? After two years ago everybody in the United States knows it."

"So your pickup was Carpenter?" I said.

She nodded. "I went back to his hotel room with him. Different men have different tastes. Some don't want to talk at all. Some like to talk sex to get them to the ready.

Carpenter wanted to know what it was like to be with two, maybe three, different guys a night. Suddenly he was ready. It—it was a little more athletic than I like it, but he didn't ask my price. He just handed me two hundred bucks and said he'd be back the next day or the day after. That was double what I usually got, you understand. Maybe more than double most times. I was waiting for him."

"And he came back?"

"The next night," she said. "We didn't have advance conversation this time. He beat me up a little, not bad, but I didn't enjoy it. This time, however, he talked afterward. He asked me if I had a pimp I was working for. I didn't. He asked me if I had a lover I went to bed with for pleasure. I told him I didn't. Finally I was giving him my life story, which was that I was trying to screw my way into some kind of a career as an actress.

" 'Maybe I can help,' he said. He told me about his job at High Crest, and how a lot of big shots in pictures came out there to ski and take lessons from him. He had some kind of Olympic medals, he said. He suggested I come out there with him and he might steer me to some guys who could do me some real good. So why not? I went. It sounded like maybe I'd hit something good."

"But it didn't turn out that way."

"Oh, God, man, how it turned out!" That fierce anger she'd first shown me came back into her blazing dark eyes. "That bastard just wanted me out there in his isolated cabin so he could play his own game of beat the drum. I could scream my head off and nobody would hear or care. He warned me that if I complained to anyone or tried to run out on him, he'd catch up with me and make me wish I'd never been born.

"Oh, he showed me off around the cocktail lounge and the dining room. And there were a lot of famous people there, just as he'd promised, but if I started to have a conversation with anyone he was always right there." She hesitated, and lifted the tips of her fingers to her face. "He —he never hit me in the face or marked me up where anyone would notice with my clothes on! That's how he threatened me. If I tried to get away from him, I wouldn't have a face left for any profession I might be in. Would you believe they're still treating me for internal injuries in this crummy joint—after two years. Pieces of a broken rib dug a hole in my gut. That—that last night he was throwing me around the cabin like a football and I—I passed out cold. When I came to, there he was, with his eyes popping out and his tongue black as a slab of licorice. You can't begin to believe how glad I was. The sonofa-bitch! It never occurred to me I'd get nailed for it, because I hadn't done it!"

I waited for her to go on, but she'd told it all. I handed her the list Nikki Chandler had supplied. "Is there anyone that you didn't notice at High Crest on this list, who might date back to some other time in your life?"

She studied it quite intently. I think she realized I was on the level and that I might be able to help her. Finally she shook her head, slowly. "There were a lot of people there who might have helped my career as an actress, but Carpenter never gave me the chance to meet them, the bastard!"

"You're positive?"

"Of course I'm positive! Wouldn't I tell you? You think I look forward to staying in this dump for the next ten years? That's how long it'll be before I come up for pa-role."

My prison guard friend appeared in the doorway. "Time's up," he said. He gave Sharon an odd look, as if he wondered how this piece of garbage could ever have been attractive to anyone in the hay. He'd certainly been listen-ing.

I had drawn a blank, except for becoming convinced that Sharon Dain had been handed a bum rap. Nora Coyle

101

had called her coarse and cheap; Mike Chandler had remarked on her distance from the right side of the tracks. Neither one of them had mentioned a a strange kind of sympathetic sadness about her.

Well, whatever she was—little mother of all the world or a cheap whore—she didn't deserve being shut away behind those grey stone walls for something she hadn't done. I could see no reason why she should be covering for anyone. The very best years of her life as a woman, her thirties, were going to be spent shut away from the world unless we could come up with something. I found I wanted to help her. Maybe what I felt explained the "Defense Committee"—something intangible about her.

The drive back to High Crest was beautiful and uneventful. What Chambrun had called my "talent" as a listener hadn't done me a damn bit of good so far. I'd listened to Mike Chandler, and Nikki, and Lance Wilson, and Sharon Dain, and I might as well have stayed back in New York making a sneaky pass at Nora Coyle. I'd developed a pretty clear picture of Hal Carpenter, a sadistic monster who'd provided a small army of people with motives for choking off his life with a length of picture wire. But the people at High Crest who'd had motives had not been in New York yesterday. The fog in which a murderer had been hidden for two years simply wouldn't clear away.

There were two people left for me to see, Jack Galt, the private eye, and Sandy Potter, the newspaper gal. Galt was waiting for me back at High Crest when my teen-age car jockey got me back there.

The detectives I knew back in New York dressed in sober business suits. I suppose, when they went under cover, they changed their appearances like chameleons to fit the world into which they moved. In the Beaumont, my world, they always reminded me of undertakers' assistants.

Jack Galt was something else—slim, blond, bright eyed

102

and gaudy. He wore plain sports slacks, white buck shoes, a gold and green shirt. A white linen sports jacket was draped over the back of a chair in the dining area where I found him. He was drinking coffee laced with brandy, which the barboy had brought him in a little glass carafe. He was a chain smoker and he'd been waiting for me for at least three butts, snuffed out in an ashtray on the table. He'd been briefed by Max Steiner, his employer at the time of Carpenter's murder, and we didn't have to go into any preliminaries.

"If Steiner had told me why you were coming before you'd started," he said, "I could have saved you the trip. I spent six months, while the trail was still hot, looking for what you're looking for. Nothing, dead end, zilch."

I sat down, ordered coffee.

"How did you find the lady?" Galt asked.

"Never having seen her before I can only guess how much she's changed," I said.

"No beauty parlors out there," Galt said.

"Nor could she make any guess about who paid her bills, Steiner's and yours, and whatever else."

Galt lit a fresh cigarette and sniffed at his coffee. "Like I said, I spent six months looking for him," he said. "Not a clue. Quite a trail, though. Little Miss Roundheels must have slept with an army of Hollywood dudes. Always looking for someone who had enough drag to give her alleged career a boost. Actress! From all accounts she had no great gifts in that direction. But what she did do well—" Gale shrugged. "I never found a sign that she ever had a permanent lover, just a long string of one-night stands that stretched out into the wild blue yonder. I don't mean she never repeated with the same customer. You ever had dealings with a professional prostitute, Haskell?"

"No business dealings," I said. I knew the call girls at the Beaumont but I'd never investigated their charms.

"The good ones are surrogate lovers," Gale said.

"Stand-ins for someone lost, someone never found. Those last two weeks with Hal Carpenter were the nearest thing to something permanent I ever found in her history."

"And that was because she was afraid to run out on him," I said.

"The more I found out about Hal Carpenter," Galt said, his voice turning tough, "the more I wished I could have spent a little time alone with him. I'd have killed the sonofabitch myself; do the world a favor."

Something was nagging at me and I remembered what it was, the list of names. I took it out of my pocket and showed it to Galt. He nodded.

"I checked out every name on that bloody list," he said.

I pointed to the name with the question mark after it —Charles Davis of Las Vegas.

"The one phony on the list," he said. "I put that question mark after his name. I was never able to locate a Charles Davis in Las Vegas. Common enough name. There are probably thousands of Charles Davises. But I couldn't find this one." He reached for a briefcase that was on the chair where he'd hung his white linen jacket. "Reams of notes on the whole damned case." He shuffled a stack of notes written on yellow, legal-size paper. Finally he found what he was looking for. "Charles Davis," he read from his notes. "One eleven Peace Street, Las Vegas, Nevada. There is no such address, by the way. I've got friends out there and no one ever heard of this guy. Mike and Nikki Chandler didn't know him. His reservation was made through a travel agent in New York City, who didn't know him either. Just a walk-in customer. He stayed here at High Crest three days, took some skiing lessons from Carpenter. He'd reserved a room for a week, but he left as soon as the cops were through questioning people after Carpenter's murder."

"Nothing fishy about him?"

"Not till much later, when I couldn't find a Charles Davis who matched High Crest's guest."

"The cops didn't spot the fact that he'd registered under a false name?"

Galt made an impatient gesture. "The cops had the case wrapped up in the first ten minutes—they thought. Sharon Dain was it. All they asked was if people had seen or heard anything. They weren't looking for anyone else. They had their pigeon. Max Steiner believed the girl and he hired me to make the only proper investigation that was made."

"And you believed her?" I asked.

"I was hired to believe her," Galt said. "I came to believe her after a while."

"This Davis. The Chandlers didn't check him out before they let him sign in?"

"My God, you don't have to show a birth certificate to register. Do they at your hotel?"

Damn near, I thought, thinking of Chambrun.

"Did this Davis have friends here, or make friends?" I asked.

"No one remembered that there was anyone obviously a friend. He chatted with a few people at the bar. Anyone you don't know at High Crest you assume is in the movie business. This Davis never said so to anyone I could find, but a couple of people got the notion that he was in the art department of one of the big studios. It didn't check out. I thought he might be connected with one of the big showcase places in Las Vegas. That didn't check out either."

"But you got a description of him?"

"I got a couple of dozen descriptions," Galt said. "Almost everyone said 'middle aged.' Depending on how old you are yourself that means anything from forty to sixty. Dark, most of them said, except for one girl who'd persuaded him to buy her a drink, who swore he was as blond as I am. Everyone wears ski clothes out here in January, just the way they wear cowboy duds here this time of year. Nothing stood out about

105

this guy. He wasn't a physical cripple for sure. Carpenter didn't teach beginners—unless they were pretty girls. You had to be in good physical shape to take lessons from him. So you have a dark, middle-aged man, who was in pretty good physical shape." Galt frowned at his notes. "This Davis told the police he came to High Crest specifically to take lessons from Carpenter. He'd heard how great he was. The only person who might have told us anything about Davis was Hal Carpenter, who was dead."

"Had you thought Davis might be the man who was paying the bills?" I asked.

"I've thought of everything there is to think of in the last eighteen months," Galt said, "but I haven't come up with a single, substantial, provable fact. I decided a while back that Davis was just an irritating red herring; some big shot who used a fake name to keep from being recognized."

The barboy came over to the table. "There's a long-distance phone call for you, Mr. Haskell," he said. "You can take it in the office, just beyond the door there."

It would be Chambrun, I thought, impatient for results. It was Betsy Ruysdale, sounding far away.

"Nothing of any consequence so far, luv," I told her.

"You're wanted back here, Mark," she said. "It's—it's happened again."

"What's happened again?" It didn't click at first.

"Another picture-wire job," Ruysdale said.

"My God! Who?" I asked.

"A stranger to us, so far," Ruysdale said. "Registered yesterday. Name of Charles Davis. Nobody here seems to know much about him."

I was staring at the phone, not believing what I heard.

"Ruysdale, listen to me," I said. "Would you believe I was just talking about a Charles Davis when your call came? He was here when Carpenter was murdered. Galt, the private eye Steiner hired, has never been

106

able to track him down. Address he gave here was a phony."

"One eleven Peace Street, Las Vegas," Ruysdale said.

"Same phony address," I said. "Same phony name."

"You'd better get back here with what you've got on this man, Mark. Chambrun is climbing the walls."

Part Three

CHAPTER ONE

Galt found it just as hard to believe my news as I had been to hear it from Ruysdale.

"The New York cops will have an advantage over me," he said. "They'll have his fingerprints. That will make a starting point I didn't have. Let me know what they come up with, Haskell. I wasted half a year trying to identify that bastard."

Getting underway wasn't dead simple. The first flight I could get from Denver was at about five o'clock. That would be seven o'clock New York time. I wouldn't get into Kennedy until shortly before midnight.

While I was waiting for the man in the office to confirm a reservation for me I got lucky. Sandy Potter found me. She was the girl reporter who'd been on my list of people to see. She wrote a sort of semigossip column for a syndicate, which appeared in most of the West Coast newspapers as *Sandra Says*. She was a breezy, uninhibited blond, wearing the in-style costume for High Crest—jeans, boots, man's shirt, and a Stetson perched on top of her golden head. She introduced herself while the man in the office was on the phone to the airport in Denver. High Crest was pretty well deserted, almost everyone having ridden up into the hills to have "caviar with the mountain goats," Mike Chandler's gag.

She came down the hall with me and perched on the edge of my bunk while I packed my bag. She'd already told the man in the office not to bother about transportation for me. She'd drive me to the airport.

"You've been talking to Jack Galt," she said.

I told her I had, and I brought her up to date on the latest news about Charles Davis. It was no secret. The media would be shouting it all over the country within the next hour. The picture-wire killer had struck for the fourth time.

She listened, frowning, and that frown made her look, somehow, like a very serious child.

"Murder isn't usually my beat," she said. "What well-known male star was seen in what famous restaurant or at what party with what glamorous lady? That's my kind of stuff. But I happened to be here two years ago, and a follow-up now is logical for me."

"Did you run across this fellow who called himself Davis?" I asked.

She shook her head. "Not to be aware of it," she said. "There were several hundred people here, top of the skiing season. I trotted out here because of Joanna Fraser's convention of liberated broads. Different from the usual. Worth a look and a listen. Then Hal Carpenter got his, and since I was on the scene my syndicate assigned me to the story."

"But Charles Davis doesn't ring a bell with you?"

"Maybe you don't know what it's like here at High Crest," she said. "It's about as informal as you can get. When you're here, you're one of the boys or one of the girls. Everyone talks to everyone. You don't bother with formal introductions. I could have had a drink at the bar with this Davis without ever bothering to find out what

112

his name was. Most of the people from Hollywood I know, at least by sight. But there were plenty of people strange to me I didn't bother to find out about. Joanna Fraser's women were my interest that week."

"Until Carpenter was strangled."

"Right. But like a good newspaperwoman I stayed close to the cops then. Sharon Dain was their only interest from the first ten minutes on, so I stayed with the Sharon Dain aspect of the case at first. Good, rich, gossip-column crud."

"Later?"

"Later I had some doubts about her guilt," Sandy said.

"Max Steiner help create those doubts?"

She shook her head. She tossed her Stetson on my bunk and fluffed out her golden hair. I had a feeling I'd like to see her out of pants and in something feminine.

"Steiner actually made me think the cops were right, at first," she said. "When you hire Max Steiner to defend you, you are most likely guilty. He gets you off with a lesser sentence. That's his particular expertise."

"But you changed your mind?"

"Not at first," she said. "But I developed a healthy sympathy for Sharon as we began to learn what kind of guy Hal Carpenter had been. Then the cops kept saying that strangling a man with picture wire was a 'woman's method.' That's just plain hooey, Mark. I can't imagine a woman thinking of doing it that way. Carpenter was an athlete, a very strong, agile man. A woman would have to be incredibly strong to slip a wire noose over his head and hold him still while he fought for his life. To plan it that way and think she could succeed just doesn't make sense to me. Never has, once I'd thought about it. I had to think it was some kind of incredible hulk of a man—powerful, relentless. Maybe these others—like Joanna Fraser—were weaklings, but not Carpenter. He would have been free of that wire, in a woman's hands, in seconds."

"You should have passed that on to Max Steiner at the time," I said.

"Oh, I did. And he agreed. You see, by then I'd decided that the cops had chosen the easy way out, and I was interesting myself in the defense committee. Steiner used my argument during the trial but the jury didn't buy it."

"You think Steiner fumbled the ball?"

"No," Sandy said, with a kind of certainty. "I think he took the only road open to him. You have no idea what the climate was like out here that January. This is 'Male Town,' Mark. Hal Carpenter was a male here, king of the ski slopes. The cops were, of course, all male. The judge was a man. The jury had ten men and only two broads— the kind you knew, from just looking at them in the jury box with the men. Papa knows best. A lot of people resented the presence of Joanna Fraser and her people. You heard talk about 'lesbians' and 'dikes.' It was almost as if the authorities wanted to show those liberated females, demanding 'equal rights,' just what equal rights really were. They'd throw the book at Sharon; just, I must admit, as they'd have thrown the book at a man who'd murdered Prince Hal. Steiner had no choice but to plead guilty and claim self-defense and temporary insanity. But evidently a prostitute didn't deserve any kind of break. If Carpenter had beat her up, and there was no question but that he had, she'd asked for it."

"But, because you didn't buy a woman using the wire method, you thought it had to be someone else—a physically powerful man?"

She nodded. "I hitched my wagon to Jack Galt about then," she said. "He's a good man at his job, Mark. He did a rundown on every single soul who was staying at High Crest at the time. The only blank he drew was this Charles Davis." She hesitated a moment, and then asked me a very shrewd question. She was no dope, that girl. "A phony name, a phony address, a disappearing act just as quickly as he could manage it. The prime suspect, you'd say, since nobody else came up hot for Jack Galt. Will you tell me, Mark, why that man for whom we've been looking for almost two years suddenly registers in your hotel in New York under that same phony name, giving the same phony address? Wasn't that a sure way for him to get himself caught?"

We looked at each other, wondering.

"Some psychos want to be caught," I said.

"But he attracted the killer, not the cops," Sandy said. "I don't get it."

There was no getting around that. Charles Davis, whoever he was, had known too much for the killer to let him live. He had been at High Crest when Carpenter was murdered. He must have seen something, heard something, known something. He hid behind that alias for almost two years and suddenly, when the killer struck again, made his presence known in or about the Beaumont, the mystery man advertising his presence and inviting his own death. As my grandfather used to say, "Try that on your pianola."

Sandy Potter drove me to the airport in Denver in a little top-down MG. She didn't need any driving lessons from Mike Chandler. We kept hashing things over on the trip, but neither of us came up with anything new that helped. She asked me to keep in touch with her. It was her story out here. I suggested she come to New York with me and get it all firsthand. For a little while there I forgot about my interest in Nora Coyle.

"Part of the story's on this end," she said. "When it's all over maybe we can celebrate, here or there."

I bought her a drink at the airport and boarded my plane. I dozed a little and drank a little and decided I'd accomplished very little on my trip. I'd formed an opinion about Sharon Dain's guilt. I had a hatful of nothing about "Charles Davis"—only that he wasn't Charles Davis. I knew that Hal Carpenter, among other things, had raped Nikki Chandler, which could have made Mike Chandler a number-one suspect, except for the fact that he had

115

certainly not been in New York when Geoffrey Hammond and Joanna Fraser were killed, and I knew exactly where he was when Charles Davis got himself garroted. Chambrun wouldn't find any of that any sort of windfall.

Just before I'd left High Crest, I'd wired Chambrun the time I was due at Kennedy. Lucky I did, because taxis were as scarce as hen's teeth, but Jerry Dodd, the Beaumont's security man, was there to meet me in one of the hotel's limousines.

Jerry looked like a man who'd been put through an old-fashioned laundry wringer. His face looked as if it might crack from fatigue.

"How did they happen to let you get away?" I asked when we got going.

"There are more cops and special guards in the hotel than customers," he said.

"Chambrun?"

"He thrives on not sleeping," Jerry said. "He's waiting up for you."

"Anything new?"

"We know who 'Charles Davis' was," he said.

That sat me up straight.

"He was a third-rate private eye with an office in Los Angeles," Jerry said. "His real name was Al Ziegler. Fingerprints got us that—FBI files. We've talked to Galt since you left High Crest. He knew this Ziegler. At least he knew who he was. He had a crummy practice, most of it involving divorce cases. He was an expert at being under the bed when some guy or doll was playing games with the wrong mate."

"So what was he doing at the Beaumont?"

"Setting himself up to be killed," Jerry said.

It seemed that other people had asked the same question Sandy Potter had asked me.

"Nothing but theory to go on," Jerry said. "The L.A. police have searched his office for us. Just one room in a crummy office building. We don't know yet where he

116

lived. But he must have kept his records in his head. Nothing about why he'd gone to New York. Nothing about High Crest two years ago. Less than a hundred bucks in a checking account, which he seems to have used only in emergencies, mainly to overdraw. His customers probably dealt with him strictly in cash. People who hire a bum like this Ziegler don't want it known. Whole damn thing is a puzzle."

"You think he was handling his specialty, some kind of a divorce thing at the Beaumont?"

"And at High Crest two years ago?" Jerry sounded angry. "He registered yesterday. This morning his registration card was on Chambrun's desk. Chambrun certainly would have known that 'Charles Davis' had pulled a disappearing act at High Crest two years ago. He was bound to be pulled in for questioning. He must have realized that."

"Maybe he didn't plan to be here that long," I said. "He was trying to attract someone else."

"He sure as hell managed that," Jerry said. "Maid found him at ten o'clock this morning when she went in to make up his room."

"Chambrun must have seen the registration cards by then," I said. "Every day, nine forty-five on the dot."

"First time in thirty years he was off schedule," Jerry said. "Hardy had him busy with something."

There was one familiar homelike thing about being back. The air, unlike High Crest's, was heavy with carbon monoxide. The Beaumont's lobby, however, wasn't like home. A dozen guys who had cop written all over them were sitting around in lobby chairs.

I headed straight up to the second floor and Chambrun's office. He was there, and Betsy Ruysdale was with him. She had no regular hours. When he was working she was working. He suggested I have a drink and I helped myself at the sideboard.

"You know we've identified 'Davis'?" he asked.

117

"Jerry told me."

"Let's have it," he said. I swear he looked just as fresh as he did at breakfast every morning. He nodded at Ruysdale. "Tape recorder, please."

When she'd switched it on, I told him all I had to tell. He never interrupted till I came to the end.

"That's all?" he asked.

"Best I could do, boss," I said.

His eyes narrowed. I couldn't tell if it was to keep out the smoke from his Egyptian cigarette or because he was angry with me.

"What did the Dain girl have to say about Geoffrey Hammond?" he asked.

I didn't remember that we'd discussed Hammond, except perhaps to mention him as one of the current victims.

"He was a man who took his pleasure from call girls," Chambrun said. "Sharon Dain was a call girl. It's not impossible their paths had crossed."

"She didn't say so. I think she would have. I mean, she got the news from me about the two jobs here."

"Call girls don't hand out their lists of customers without some urging." Chambrun sounded impatient. "You had noticed a habit Hammond and Hal Carpenter had in common? Your girl here in the Beaumont with a black eye, Sharon Dain with her broken ribs, and your Nikki Chandler, violently raped. A couple of strong-arm sex goons, just asking for trouble."

"But that doesn't tie in with Joanna Fraser," I said. "I wasn't interested in bedroom gossip. I was looking for someone who cared enough for Sharon Dain to kill her persecutor and anyone else who'd turned his back on her. Someone with a hell of a lot of money to throw around to defend her."

"And you came up with 'Charles Davis,'" Chambrun said. He sounded disgusted. "A cheap private eye with less than a hundred bucks in the bank. I ought to ask you

118

to pay your own expenses to High Crest."

"So I goofed," I said. "I'm sorry. What next?"

Chambrun reached for the demitasse of Turkish coffee Ruysdale kept filled at his desk. He suddenly looked tired. "I'm sorry, Mark," he said. "I'm really burned up with myself. We haven't done any better on this end than you did out there. We found out who 'Davis' really was. That's all. And we found that out too late."

I felt myself relaxing. There wasn't an unfair bone in Chambrun's body. That was why any of us who worked for him would go out on the farthest limb to please him.

"You put what pieces you have together and you don't come out with much," he said. "Take a look at it, Mark. You may see something that I don't."

Not much chance of that, I thought, as I waited for him to go on after he'd lit a fresh cigarette. I noticed Ruysdale hadn't turned off the tape recorder.

"Let's take this Al Ziegler," he said. "He goes to High Crest two years ago and registers as 'Charles Davis' from One eleven Peace Street, Las Vegas. He doesn't go there for a holiday. He doesn't have that kind of private money. He's on a job, and a client is paying his expenses. He takes skiing lessons from Hal Capenter, also an expense. Was Carpenter his reason for being there, or was that just a cover to make it look as if he had a genuine reason for vacationing at High Crest? His track record would indicate he was there to catch some guy playing games with the wrong woman, or some gal there with the wrong man. Grounds for divorce. So that's one missing answer. We don't know if Carpenter had a connection with Ziegler's case. He wasn't married. He was shacked up with a prostitute, not someone's wife."

"Certainly no divorce angle there," I said.

"But we can't be certain he was on a divorce case. He would take any kind of job, I'd guess, for the right kind of fee. A client who would pay his freight at High Crest wasn't broke. So, as I said, that is one missing piece.

"Three days after Ziegler-Davis arrives at High Crest, Carpenter is murdered. The cops are very casual about questioning the guests. They are fixed on Sharon Dain. Ziegler gets out of there as fast as he can, because if they should eventually check up on 'Charles Davis,' they might discover who he was. Private investigators aren't popular with the cops and they might try to force him to tell who he was working for and why.

"At that point 'Davis' turns back into Ziegler. The L.A. cops tell us he was working at his regular job for the last two years, perfectly visible in his office until a couple of days ago. Then he comes here and 'Charles Davis' is re-born. Why?"

"It doesn't make sense," I said. "He was running the risk of your uncovering his whole charade."

"It made sense to him," Chambrun said. "That's another missing piece."

"If he left Los Angeles two days ago, that was before the killer struck at Hammond and Mrs. Fraser," I said. "No connection."

"But 'Charles Davis' reborn after two years makes a connection," Chambrun said. "Maybe he came to New York on some legitimate case and heard the news about the killings here after he arrived. Suggest anything to you, Mark?"

"Carpenter's killer was at it again. He'd know that."

"So Ziegler advertises his presence by registering as 'Charles Davis.' But who would see the advertisement? This isn't fifty years ago. Our guests don't register in one big book so that the next guest can see who's registered ahead of him. Each guest signs a separate card, the room clerk files it away. No way for anyone else to see it unless he was standing right there when Ziegler signed in. The room clerk might say, audibly, 'Your room is six-oh-four, Mr. Davis.' Aside from that, there's no way for anyone outside the staff to know who's registered and in what room."

"And did that happen?"

"I don't know," Chambrun said. "Things were pretty hectic, people checking out, asking questions. It isn't reasonable for Atterbury, or anyone else on the desk, to remember a small thing like that. They don't. There's only one thing on the 'Davis' card that distinguishes it from the usual. He didn't have any luggage. He told Atterbury he'd missed his plane to the coast and his bags were at the airport. He paid cash in advance for his room. We had so many people checking out that there were rooms. It's not so unheard-of that Atterbury had any reason to hesitate."

"He didn't intend to stay long," I said. "You'd be likely to spot him when you saw the cards this morning."

"Could he know that?"

"With everyone in the hotel being checked over by the police? He'd have to know it was possible," I said.

Chambrun leaned back in his chair, his eyelids lowered. "You want to hear a wild theory?" he asked.

"If it's your theory it may not be so wild," I said.

"Wild. Far out," he said. "But it could be." He drew a deep breath. "Let's go back two years. Ziegler is hired to go to High Crest to look for someone or to spy on someone. *But he doesn't know who his client is.* He's hired over the phone, the name wouldn't mean anything if a name was given. Expense money delivered in cash by mail or by messenger. Ziegler goes to High Crest and registers as 'Davis.' Carpenter is murdered, and Ziegler has reason to believe his client is the killer. *But he doesn't know who he is!*"

"That is wild," I said.

"If he was hired to look for Sharon Dain and find out what she was up to?"

"Oh, brother!" I said.

"For two years Ziegler tries to track down that client. Why? Because that client obviously had money and Ziegler's silence could be worth a good chunk of it."

"Not so wild," I said.

"Then the killer strikes again here, after two years. It's all over radio and television and the papers. Ziegler, in New York on some other business, guesses that his client is in or around the Beaumont. He can't finger him because he has no idea who he is or what he looks like. But maybe he can draw the killer to him. The name 'Charles Davis' would do it. Ziegler expects the man to come to him and pay for his silence. It works, except that the man comes with a length of picture wire in his pocket."

"Wouldn't Ziegler be prepared for that?"

"Maybe. Also—maybe—he left his room and circulated around the lobby, hoping the killer would spot him if the registration gimmick didn't work. The killer has spotted him, one way or the other, gets into Ziegler's room while Ziegler is out of it, and is standing behind the door when Ziegler comes back, wire noose at the ready."

"No struggle?" I asked.

"The body was found just inside the door of six-oh-four," Chambrun said. "The maid actually couldn't get the door wide open because the body blocked it. He was caught from behind, like the others, and it was over almost before he knew what was happening to him."

"Was the door to six-oh-four forced?"

"No. But all the killer had to do was stop at the desk and ask for the key to six-oh-four. In all the confusion nobody asked him for any ID." Chambrun opened his eyes wide. "Add up to anything like sense to you, Mark?"

"It could be. It could very well be," I said.

"And it's no more than a conversation piece," he said, impatient again. "We're no closer to guessing who the killer is, who Ziegler's client was two years ago." He gestured to Ruysdale to turn off the tape recorder. "Play that for Hardy next time he shows up here," he said.

"So where do we stand?" I asked him.

"In total confusion," he said. "The hotel is swarming with cops, special guards, and the press. In the bars, the restaurants, the shops, people don't talk about anything else. Somebody sees some lonely guy wandering around the corridors and they run screaming for help—if the guy doesn't start screaming for help first. It's mad. We've got special guards thrown around people who may have had even the remotest connection with High Crest two years ago—Alvin Parker, Bobby Bryan, your Miss Coyle. Hardy has cops watching Roy Conklin at his apartment and office, Colin Dobler at his Gramercy Park studio, and Max Steiner at his apartment and office. There may be other people right here in this hotel, but no one has come forward to say they were at High Crest. Hardy got the list of guests at High Crest two years ago from the police out there—the one you saw with the question mark after the name Charles Davis. So far, Alvin Parker and Nora Coyle are the only people staying here at the Beaumont who are on that list. As you know, neither Roy Conklin nor Colin Dobler are on it. Nor Bobby Bryan. Just to cheer you, I can't see your Miss Coyle as the physically powerful killer of three strong, agile men—Carpenter, Hammond, and Ziegler."

"She'll be glad to hear it," I said. "You still think Hammond and Joanna Fraser were done in just because they refused to help Sharon Dain?"

"How can we possibly be sure of anything until we know who the killer is?" Chambrun said. "My invention about Ziegler and his client explains why the killer waited two years to go after him. But if Geoffrey Hammond and Joanna Fraser knew something that would incriminate Carpenter's killer, why would they have kept it to themselves for two years? The original theory that the killer waited for two years till all Sharon Dain's appeals had been exhausted and then went after people who had refused her is as good as any." Chambrun pushed back his chair and stood up. "Max Steiner is coming here for breakfast, nine o'clock. I'd like you present, Mark. Get what sleep you can."

123

"You think Steiner can be helpful?"

"He's spent two years on the Dain case, hasn't he? And God help us, Mark, if the Dain case isn't at the core of this we're really lost."

I went down the hall to my apartment. I unlocked the door and went into the dark living room. I'd only taken two steps into the room when someone grabbed me from behind.

"Stand just where you are, buster," a harsh voice said.

I felt something like a gun jammed into my back, and for one moment, so ghastly I can't describe it, I expected to be fitted with a wire collar.

Then the living room lights were switched on. The man behind me was slapping me over for a weapon of some sort. Nora Coyle appeared in the door to my bedroom, wearing some kind of a thin, see-through nightgown.

"Thank God, Mark!" she said. "It's all right, officer. It's Mr. Haskell and this is his apartment."

I turned to face a grim-faced cop. "Sorry," he said. "Didn't they tell you the lady was being guarded? You should have identified yourself before walking in like that."

I felt ten years older.

CHAPTER TWO

I didn't get much sleep that night. The cop sat down in his chair by the door. He wasn't going anywhere.

I went into the bedroom with Nora. She climbed back into bed and sat there, a sheet pulled up around her. I had to tell her about my trip, everything I'd found out and had heard from Chambrun. I remember I went out to the kitchenette and made drinks. I offered the cop one, but

124

he asked for a rain check for when he was off duty.

I don't know how long we talked, a couple of hours I'd guess. I said something about not wanting to sleep on the couch with the cop watching me. Would you believe that eventually I slept beside Nora in my bed and never touched her? Unless I stroked her in my sleep.

I have some kind of inner alarm clock that wakes me for that daily breakfast meeting with Chambrun. Nora was sleeping like a happy, healthy child. She didn't stir when I went into the bathroom, shaved and showered, and dressed for the day. I made coffee and discovered that there was a different cop at the front door. The relief man was cut out of the same pattern. He thanked me for coffee as I left to go down the hall to Chambrun's office.

It was the same as always there. The breakfast buffet was laid out, with Monsieur Fresney, the chef, presiding. Max Steiner, the lawyer, small, grey, bubbling with energy, was just as I'd pictured him. The cop I'd seen in Ruysdale's outer office was evidently his bodyguard. Steiner said hello to me. He'd evidently been listening to the tape Chambrun had made of his "wild theory" the night before.

"Ingenious," Steiner said. "Quite possible. All you need to do is prove it. If I'd been able to spot Ziegler two years ago, I might have got Sharon off. Sonofabitch sat on what he knew and let them railroad her."

"If there's any truth in my dream-up," Chambrun said, "he couldn't have helped you much. He didn't know who his client was."

"But he could have forced the cops to look for that client," Steiner said. "It would have injected someone else into the case. That's all I needed at the time."

Steiner selected eggs and bacon for his breakfast. Chambrun chose a filet mignon, with his usual gluten toast, sweet butter, and wild strawberry jam. I had chicken hash. Chambrun had taught me to develop a taste for it.

125

"How long am I going to be followed around by these bodyguards?" Steiner asked, when we had got to our second cups of coffee and cigarettes.

"Till you're safe," Chambrun said.

"You're still buying this theory of a psycho who's going to punish everyone who failed Sharon?" Steiner asked.

"I don't know what I'm buying," Chambrun said. "Anyone connected with the case, no matter how remotely, needs protection until we know more than we do. No one could have been any more remote than Geoffrey Hammond. He wasn't at High Crest. He didn't know Sharon Dain—or did he?"

"Not so far as I know," Steiner said.

"You asked him to interview her and he turned you down?"

Steiner made a hopeless gesture with his expressive small hands. "We were just approaching the trial by then," he said. "Two months after the murder. Hammond owed me, in a way. I thought he might be willing to pay off."

"Owed you?"

"Some years ago he did a show on the failure of the courts to handle crime in the big cities. Courts overcrowded. Plea bargaining. Only five percent of the people charged with felonies ever go to jail. He was to interview a couple of judges, a couple of big city prosecutors. He wanted to be primed with the right kind of questions to ask. He came to me. I gave him the ammunition he needed. He offered to pay me a fee for my time, but I told him it was on the house. I was interested in seeing our court system get the business. But I suggested that some day I might want a favor from him."

"And Sharon Dain was that favor?"

Steiner nodded. "He had to turn me down. You see, the interview with Sharon would have had to take place before she went on trial. That was about three weeks away when I called him from High Crest and asked him. There

126

was no way he could fit it into his schedule. Time was already bought, advertisers lined up for interviews he'd already taped. No way to slide in a different show. His contracts wouldn't permit it. He didn't turn me down because he thought it wouldn't make a good show, or because he had any sort of prejudice against Sharon Dain. He just couldn't handle it."

"As far as you know he'd never met her? He was interested in her kind of woman. Girls in the hotel here knew him on that basis."

"Certainly he never suggested it, nor did I think of it," Steiner said.

"And Joanna Fraser. You went to her, too, for help, didn't you?"

"That was in the very beginning, when I first came on the case," Steiner said. "She was there at High Crest, with her convention of liberated dolls. It was one of the people on the defense committee, a young movie actor named Lance Wilson, who suggested that a statement from Joanna Fraser might be useful. I wanted the case tried somewhere else. High Crest was what you might call a man's town."

I'd heard that before from Sandy Potter.

"I thought Sharon would have a better chance in some other climate," Steiner said. "Wilson went to the Fraser woman's secretary."

"Nora Coyle," Chambrun said. He glanced at me. "She's here in the hotel now, with bodyguards like you, Steiner."

"Mrs. Fraser had refused to talk to me or to Wilson, but Wilson managed to charm Miss Coyle into presenting our case. She came back with a not-too-unreasonable answer from Joanna Fraser. Fraser thought her getting into the act might do Sharon Dain more harm than good. The prejudice out there in the Colorado mountains against the 'liberated female' as a political entity was high. If she took some kind of public stand in support of Sharon, it could

127

very well hurt instead of help. To show that she wasn't just brushing us off she contributed five hundred dollars to the defense fund."

"Nora never mentioned that," I said, "or Colin Dobler either, so far as I know."

Steiner chuckled. "Joanna Fraser was really liberated," he said. "I think she didn't want to show support for Sharon for the reason she gave. So she didn't tell anyone, not even her secretary or her ex-husband, that she'd sent me a cash contribution with the request that it not be made public. That lady lived her own life in her own way. I dare say no one close to her knew all there was to know about her." The little grey lawyer made an impatient gesture. "There's a question I keep asking myself."

"So ask us," Chambrun said.

"I'm not a psychiatrist," Steiner said, "but in my time I've had a lot to do with psychotic criminals. There often aren't rational explanations for their behavior. You people have come up with an explanation for this killer's irrational behavior. He killed Hammond and Joanna Fraser, you think, because they refused to help Sharon Dain. Now you come up with something a lot solider to explain why he killed 'Charles Davis.' Fear of exposure. But tell me this, gentlemen, if he wanted to punish the people responsible for Sharon Dain's conviction, why pick on a man who couldn't schedule a public interview in time to be useful, and why pick on a woman who sympathized with Sharon, contributed to her defense fund, and refused public support only because she felt it might damage Sharon's chances? So help me, that's reaching, even for a disturbed mind. Why not go after the judge who presided at the trial and whose rulings and eventual summing up to the jury were incredibly prejudiced? Why not go after the prosecutor who smeared Sharon from one end of the country to the other, damned her for her life-style, nailed her on purely circumstantial evidence? Why not go after the investigators for the state police, who built up that circumstantial case and refused to look anywhere else for any other possible killer? Why not the jury? Why not the local press who tried and convicted Sharon Dain before she ever went to court? Aren't those the logical targets for some kind of a nut out to get revenge for Sharon?"

"Logical for a logical mind," Chambrun said. "We're not dealing with a logical mind."

"Who says?" Steiner asked. "If you're right, he had a logical reason for silencing Ziegler-Davis. Has anyone thought of looking for more logical reasons for eliminating Hammond and Joanna Fraser than some vague, two-year's delayed reprisal because they didn't help? Haven't you and the cops just grabbed at an easy explanation, Mr. Chambrun?"

Chambrun sat very still, his eyes narrowed against the smoke from his cigarette.

"I think you've let yourselves be mesmerized by the first concept you came up with on the workings of a deranged mind," Steiner said. "The motive for the murders of Hammond and Joanna Fraser may be a lot more rational than you've let yourselves believe. You had to come up with something realistic in the Ziegler-Davis case because that didn't fit your starting theory about the others. Wouldn't it be worthwhile to look for something more realistic to explain the first two cases? I say you've let yourselves be handcuffed by your first, entirely invented concept of the workings of a psychotic mind. I suggest you get off your butts and look for real motives."

Chambrun reached for the ashtray beside his place and snubbed out his cigarette. I knew him well enough to recognize that Steiner had rung a bell with him.

"If I ever get into trouble with the law, Mr. Steiner," Chambrun said, "I'd like to put in a bid, now, for your services."

Steiner laughed. "Flattery will get you everything," he said.

"It's not flattery, because of course you're right," Chambrun said.

There was a council of war later that morning, with Lieutenant Hardy representing the police, Nora Coyle and Colin Dobler from the Fraser camp, and Bobby Bryan and Roy Conklin, the people closest to Geoffrey Hammond. Alvin Parker was there, neat as always. I suppose you could say that Betsy Ruysdale, Jerry Dodd, and I represented Chambrun and the hotel.

Chambrun laid Steiner's case on the line to them.

"It can be that we've been accepting an easy explanation," he said at the end. "Someone—perhaps I—suggested it and we haven't bothered to look for anything else, just as the police in High Crest refused to look for another suspect in the Carpenter murder. Max Steiner made his point to me. I want to make it to you. Somewhere, unconsciously buried in your minds for the last two years, may be the real motives that will lead us to the killer."

Roy Conklin lurched up out of his chair and limped over toward the windows on his aluminum leg. "Damned meddling amateur," he said under his breath.

Chambrun looked as though he hadn't heard.

Colin Dobler, Joanna Fraser's ex-husband, spoke in his low, quiet voice. "You have to rub two sticks together to strike a spark," he said. "Or a match and a striking surface. Our problem is that we have nothing to relate to, no striking surface. Tell us whom you suspect, Mr. Chambrun, and that might kindle some helpful memory."

"We don't have any genuine suspect, Mr. Dobler," Hardy said.

"So you're protecting us from a phantom!" Conklin said from the window in his harsh, angry voice.

"You want protection, don't you, Mr. Conklin?" Hardy asked.

130

"What the hell good is it if you don't know from whom or what you're protecting us?"

"Oh, we know what, Mr. Conklin. We're protecting you from a man with a coil of picture wire in his pocket," Hardy said.

I could almost sense a kind of controlled panic in the room. Somewhere—around the next corner—a killer could be waiting for one of them. I remembered Nora's enormous relief, earlier on, when she saw that it was me and not the killer that cop had cornered in my apartment. They were all living with it every second, no matter how cool they appeared on the surface.

"Colin's right, of course," Nora said. "We have nothing to relate to, no way to get started thinking the way you want us to, Mr. Chambrun."

"There isn't time for us to get involved in any kind of free-associating group analysis," Chambrun said. "You have to go back two years. Some of you were at High Crest when Hal Carpenter was murdered, some of you weren't."

"Miss Coyle and I were there," Alvin Parker said.

I'd forgotten to ask anyone how the ball to raise funds for the Parker Foundation had gone. Neatly, I guessed. And while it was going on, Ziegler-Davis was being choked to death in 604. All these people had been somewhere in the neighborhood when that was happening.

"You can tell us more about High Crest than anyone else, Mr. Parker," Chambrun said. "You understand how they operated, you saw their books, you circulated with the guests. Try to think of anything you can remember, no matter how far removed from the murder, that might touch Joanna Fraser or Geoffrey Hammond. Anything that might connect them in any way with High Crest, with Sharon Dain, with Hal Carpenter."

"Of course Joanna Fraser and Miss Coyle were there," Parker said.

"There may be something one of you has forgotten to tell because it didn't seem important. Let us decide what

131

has value and what hasn't. You, too, Mr. Dobler—any conversation you ever had with Joanna Fraser that related to High Crest, or Sharon Dain, or Hal Carpenter. There were two years in which she must have talked any number of times about what happened at High Crest. The trial, the appeals, have been on television, radio, in the newspapers. Anything she ever said, no matter how casual and unimportant it seemed at the time, may be important now."

Bobby Bryan spoke for the Hammond forces. "Roy and I both knew at that time, two years ago, that Max Steiner had tried to talk Geoff into interviewing the Dain girl on television. It would have been done as a favor to Steiner —if it could have been done. Geoff wasn't interested in murder cases, crime stories. He was a political animal. But he owed Steiner for past help on one of his shows, and he might have considered repaying that debt if he could have. He would have had to interview the girl before she went to trial. There just wasn't a slot where he could fit her in." He shrugged. "I can't remember Geoff ever mentioning the case. He wasn't involved, so he wasn't interested. He may not even have known how the trial came out."

Roy Conklin limped a step or two toward us from the windows. "And one thing's for sure," he said. "Geoff Hammond wasn't in High Crest at the time, or anywhere else in Colorado." He reached in his pocket and pulled out a folded sheet of paper. "I went through some files in my office after—after yesterday. The night Harold Carpenter was murdered, Geoff—and you, Bobby, in case you've forgotten—were in Geneva, Switzerland. You didn't come back to this country until ten days later. Steiner didn't get in touch with Geoff until a month after that."

"Of course," Bobby said. "I had forgotten."

"And you, Mr. Conklin?" Chambrun said.

"I, if it's any of your business," Conklin said, "was here in New York, minding the store, so to speak. I have other clients beside Geoff Hammond. Perhaps the Lieutenant would like to see my appointment book for that period of time—if I can find it. That was two years ago, for God sake!"

Lieutenant Hardy didn't look like a happy man. "I'm just a policeman," he said, "trying to do a complicated job." He sounded on the edge of anger. "I find your theories and Steiner's fascinating, Pierre; who remembers what two years ago. It might get us some new theories if anyone remembers anything more interesting than anything we've got now. But there is a hell of a better way to get to the core of this thing."

"Tell us, Walter," Chambrun said.

"Who had breakfast with Geoffrey Hammond day before yesterday? Who had cocktails with Joanna Fraser before luncheon that same day? Unless we're dealing with a gang of killers, which I doubt, it was the same person. You, Bryan, and you, Conklin, what about the breakfast guest? And you, Miss Coyle, and you, Dobler, what about the cocktail guest?"

"I've already told you—" Bobby began.

"I know what you've told me," Hardy interrupted. "He didn't tell you whom he'd invited for breakfast. But who *could* it have been? Conklin thought it was you, that you often breakfasted with Hammond."

"But not that day," Bobby said. It had the flat ring of truth to it.

"So think," Hardy said. "You don't invite a casual stranger to breakfast. It didn't just happen by chance. It was arranged for. Hammond ordered breakfast for two from room service. What close friends might fit the picture? What business associates? Could it have been one of those Palestinian people he was about to interview?"

"It couldn't have been an unexpected, casual drop-in, Bryan," Chambrun said. "Hammond was registered here in Conklin's name, he was under cover, not circulating in the hotel. No one was supposed to know he was here. Right?"

Bobby nodded.

"So he must have invited someone," Hardy said. "Who? Who would he be likely to invite."

"So help me, I haven't the remotest idea," Bobby said.

Hardy turned to a glowering Roy Conklin. "You?" he said.

"I told you, I'd assumed it was Bobby. That the killer came in after Bobby had left. But if it wasn't Bobby—no notion," Conklin said.

Hardy looked to be near the end of his patience. He turned to Colin Dobler. "About Joanna Fraser's cocktail companion?"

Dobler answered in that slow way of his. "My relationship with Joanna was not altogether usual," he said. "You could say it was periodic. We were divorced six years ago. That was when Joanna went into her liberation kick and a husband became something of an albatross."

"A what?" Hardy asked.

"An albatross—hung around her neck. Old legend?" Dobler gave the detective a gentle smile. "In her way, in short. But we remained very good friends. Something more than good friends, I guess you'd say." He glanced at Nora. "Miss Coyle has told you, or will if you ask her the right questions, that there were times when Joanna still needed me—shall we say for romantic reasons? On those occasions, if they took place here in her apartment, Miss Coyle, who had a room in it, was asked to—to go somewhere else. But day before yesterday, unfortunately, was not one of the times when my presence was required."

"Unfortunately?"

"Because if I had been here Joanna would be alive," Dobler said. "I have no idea who was here for cocktails, not the remotest. I was at work in my studio on Gramercy Park."

"Witness to that?" Hardy asked.

134

"I don't have an audience when I'm working, Lieutenant."

Hardy turned to Nora. He didn't have to ask her the question.

"As Colin has told you, we weren't in one of Joanna's romantic periods," she said. "I spent the night before in my own room in her apartment. I had breakfast with her. At about eleven in the morning I went out to do some personal shopping for her. I came back a little after one and—and found her."

"She didn't tell you someone was coming for cocktails?"

"No. I think you might call that unusual if it was planned ahead of time. Just in passing she'd have said so-and-so is stopping by for drinks before lunch. But bear in mind, Lieutenant, she wasn't in hiding like Mr. Hammond. She lived here. Hundreds of her friends knew that. Any one of them could have called her from the lobby and Joanna would have invited them up."

"We think this has to have been a man," Hardy said.

"Being a liberated woman doesn't mean you don't have men friends," Nora said. "There wasn't a room service order, so it couldn't have been a stranger. She made the martinis herself."

"Best in the world," Dobler said. "Made with loving care."

"All I'm saying is that her guest must have been unexpected, but a friend," Nora said.

"A deadly friend," Chambrun said. "Were there other men who shared her romantic moments, in addition to Mr. Dobler, Nora?"

Nora hesitated. "I can only tell you there was no one else I knew about. No one who came here. I was never asked to leave except when Colin was to be her guest. Her relationship with Colin was no secret to any of her friends."

"She could be a very private person," Dobler said, "if she chose."

"Did you think there was another man or men?" Chambrun asked.

Dobler gave him a gentle smile. "You're wondering if I killed her in a fit of jealousy? But the Lieutenant doesn't think you're dealing with a gang of killers. Was I jealous of Hammond? Joanna didn't like his public image, but she didn't know him. I didn't know him. If there was another man—and I say if—it surely wasn't Hammond."

We sat or stood around the office, looking at each other. Like every road we traveled, this one, too, turned out to be a dead end.

"So we go about it another way," Hardy said. He focused on Chambrun. "The long, tedious way, not so imaginative as yours, Pierre. We question every bellhop, every elevator operator. We talk to every maid and housekeeper on Hammond's floor and Joanna Fraser's floor. We talk to the guests on those floors. Who did anyone see around eight o'clock on Hammond's floor, after eleven on Joanna Fraser's floor? It can take forever, but we may come up with two descriptions that fit the same person. There may be something distinctive about this crazy bastard that more than one person will remember. Meanwhile I urge you all to try to come up with some kind of guesses that could be an answer, no matter how far-fetched."

He turned, beckoning to Jerry Dodd to follow him, and walked out of the office. It would be Jerry's job to talk to dozens of people, who had probably seen nothing.

I managed to convey to Nora that I'd join her in my place, but I stayed behind, as they all left, to get my instructions from Chambrun. He sat behind his desk, motionless, not answering the vague good-byes as a handful of frightened people left us.

"I don't envy them," I said, trying to break the ice. "It must not be fun to know that this psycho is around some-

136

where and that you, without knowing why, may be next on his list."

Chambrun gave me that level stare of his that always seemed to be the prelude to telling me that I was not far removed from being an idiot.

"Steiner made his point with me," he said, flat and impersonal. "You get on this man's list for some perfectly understandable reason. I think if there is someone else on it he knows."

"And doesn't tell us?"

"Can't tell us because of what that would reveal about him," Chambrun said. He reached, automatically, for his little cup of Turkish coffee. I almost shuddered when he lifted it to his lips. I can't stand the taste of it myself. He put down the cup, looking at me as if I were a stranger.

"We will, sooner or later, close in on this man—by luck, or by Hardy's slow plodding. When we get near him, you, I, Jerry Dodd, or Hardy may find himself on that list."

"Me?" I said, startled.

"He doesn't know what you may have found out at High Crest."

"But nothing!" I protested.

"Who knows, when it's put together with something else we may find?" Chambrun said. "This man doesn't mean to be caught, Mark. Whether he kills four times or a dozen can't matter very much to him. He's already accumulated more penalties than he can pay in a lifetime. No one who gets in his way is safe. So don't feel too smugly superior to those people who just left us. Don't be careless. Don't turn your back on anyone. We're all in the same boat as far as this monster is concerned."

CHAPTER THREE

There is a line I've heard Chambrun speak many times. We on the staff will go to him with some kind of problem, some kind of crisis. Let me say, parenthetically, that we didn't face the kind of crisis we had that day very often. Chambrun will listen for just as long as it takes him to assimilate all the facts, and then he will put an end to the conversation by saying, "Let's not forget we still have a hotel to run."

After his not so gentle warning to me, Chambrun had the Beaumont on his mind.

"I want you to circulate, Mark," he said. "Do what you can to calm down our special guests. Not everyone is in the same kind of danger that we are. Try to persuade the press people you know that we don't need an army of self-appointed detectives trying to solve the case. Promise them facts when we have facts. Meanwhile get them to back off if you can."

"Not much hope of that," I said.

"Try being charming," Chambrun said drily. "But above all, Mark, listen! Listen to any gossip, any wild notions anyone has. Most of all, listen to anything anyone on the staff has to say. They're more likely to talk to you than to Hardy and his people. Who saw anyone on Hammond's floor around breakfast time, on Joanna Fraser's floor at lunchtime? It's just possible we have a witness who doesn't realize that he, or she, is a witness."

"Witness to what?" I asked.

"Witness to the presence of the same person in both those places at those different times," Chambrun said. "The breakfast guest at Hammond's and the cocktail guest at Joanna Fraser's has to have been the same person. Our man. If he was seen in those areas by different people, there may be a description that will come together into one picture."

"Isn't that what Hardy and Jerry are working at?" I asked.

He smiled, a tight little smile. "Sit a frightened maid down in front of a grim policeman and she's likely to forget her own name," he said. "You're friends with the staff. They trust you. Listen to what they're talking about."

If there is someone you love who is trying to hide the fact that she isn't well, you will know it no matter what kind of a front she puts up. That's how it was in the Beaumont that noontime. On the surface everything seemed to be running with its usual efficiency, staff people on their jobs where they should be, waiters and maitre d's at their posts, doormen and bellhops functioning as usual, Atterbury and his people at the front desk the usual smiling hosts. But under the surface I sensed the tensions that were there. There were more unfamiliar faces than I could ever remember seeing—cops, special guards, men and women I guessed were reporters who didn't usually cover the Beaumont, and just plain rubberneckers hanging around waiting for something to happen.

All I had to do to be swamped by both friends and strangers was to appear in the lobby. All there was to listen to were questions I couldn't, or wouldn't answer. I felt like some movie star being swarmed over by autograph hunters. I invented a kind of frozen smile that I gave to everyone.

"I'm sorry—I can't tell you anything till the police are ready to make a statement—I'm sorry—I'm afraid I have no comment to make on that." Over and over.

On the fringe of the crowd I saw my friend Dick Barrows, the crime reporter for the *Times,* giving me a sardonic look. I finally worked my way to where he was standing.

"I thought you were my pal, Mark," he said.

"Things have happened so fast," I said. "Did you know I've been to Colorado and back?"

"I knew you were missing. Look, Mark, you can't turn us off, you know."

"Orders from Chambrun and Hardy," I said.

"Where can I find Guido Maroni?" he asked.

"Who the hell is Guido Maroni?"

"Don't play games with me, Mark. He's the room service waiter who served Hammond's breakfast the morning he was murdered."

I had never known the little Italian waiter's full name.

"What about him?" I asked.

"Didn't you know he hasn't come to work the last two mornings?"

I hadn't known. I knew he'd been grilled by Hardy's people that first day and had nothing to report. He'd brought the breakfast wagon, Hammond had told him where to leave it, and he'd come back two hours later and found Hammond strangled.

"They most likely gave him time off," I said. "He was probably in shock after what he saw. I would have been."

"You saw, and you weren't given time off," Barrows said.

"I'm not a hysterical waiter," I said. "I didn't have to serve meals to hotel guests with shaking hands."

"I want to talk to him," Barrows said. "How do I find him?"

And before I could interrupt he went on. "I'm working alone, Mark. But if you don't tell me how to find Maroni, I'll have the whole damned press corps looking for him."

"Why do you want him?"

"I want the same information you want, maybe have already got. Who was the breakfast guest? Did Maroni see anyone in the hall, anywhere, who might have been?"

This smart reporter was working the same beat we were. He could clutter us up badly if he called in the rest of the newshounds.

140

"The personnel manager will have his address," I said. "I'll see what I can do for you."

Bill Wheaton, the PM, wasn't as cooperative as I'd expected.

"Hardy's been asking for the same information," he said. "I don't think I can give it to you, Mark, without his permission. Certainly not for Dick Barrows."

"He'll turn the place upside down if we shut him out," I said.

"Ask Hardy," Bill said.

"Guido was given time off?" I asked.

Bill shook his head. "When he didn't come in the next day, we just assumed he was too shaken up," he said. "When he failed to show this morning, we called his home. Now this is just for you, Mark, not for anyone else. Not for Barrows, for sure."

I nodded.

"We got Guido's wife on the phone. She's in a state. He's been missing since the late afternoon of the murders. He went out to buy a newspaper. He wasn't satisfied with what came over his TV set. He didn't come back and there hasn't been any word from him."

Lieutenant Hardy had taken over what we call the executive room on the lobby level. You can bring your board of directors there and seat them around a long, narrow table. I found Hardy talking with one of the maids from the thirty-fourth floor, along with Mrs. Kniffin, the head housekeeper. I guessed Mrs. Kniffin wasn't going to have the police questioning "my girls" unless she was there to protect them. Maybe I was pooping out, because the three of them looked a long way off at the far end of the table, almost like a distorted camera angle. I signaled to Hardy and he came down the room, rather reluctantly I thought, to join me. I assumed Jerry Dodd was rounding up other personnel for questioning.

"Dick Barrows of the *Times* is looking for Guido Maroni," I said.

"Damn!" Hardy said.

"If we don't tell him something, he'll have the thundering herd down on us, Lieutenant. What is there we can tell him? He knows Guido hasn't turned up for work for two days."

"I didn't know that myself till half an hour ago," Hardy said. "I've sent Sergeant Baxter uptown to talk to Mrs. Maroni."

"What do you think can have happened to him?"

"Probably the center of attention in his neighborhood. He found a murdered man. His friends spotted him when he went out to buy a paper, persuaded him to tell them his story, plied him with some good red wine. He's probably sleeping it off somewhere. Baxter will find him when Mrs. Maroni tells him who Guido's friends are."

I didn't think Hardy spoke with any real conviction.

"You believe that?" I asked.

"I hope," he said, frowning.

"You think—?"

"The man we're looking for could have found him," Hardy said. "If Guido could recognize him, saw him on Hammond's floor that morning, he might have to be silenced."

"God!" I said.

"We have a way of thinking melodramatic thoughts just about now," Hardy said. "I hope the first explanation is nearer the truth."

"What do I do with Dick Barrows?"

"Shove him down the nearest laundry chute," Hardy said.

"Seriously, pal," I said. "If you let him in on this, he may be willing to hold his fire until you say the word."

Hardy nodded. "I'll talk to him," he said.

I found Dick Barrows in the lobby where I'd left him.

"I was beginning to think you'd hung me out to dry," he said.

"Talk to Hardy. Play it his way," I said. "Don't try to put the heat on him. He doesn't like heat."

"Does he know where Guido Maroni is?"

"He'll tell you," I said.

So much for the problem of Dick Barrows. What to tell him would be Hardy's decision.

I decided to take a swing up to the Trapeze Bar. There would probably be more regulars up there than down on the lobby floor. Almost the first people I saw as I walked into the Trapeze were Bobby Bryan and Roy Conklin, Hammond's secretary and his business manager, sitting at a corner table. A waiter was just delivering what appeared to be at least their second drinks. He was removing empty glasses before he put down the current order. Bobby spotted me and waved to me to join them. Two men sitting at the bar watched me closely as I crossed the room. Police body-guards I guessed.

"Martinis help stimulate your memories?" I asked, as I sat down in a chair the waiter pulled up for me.

"Goddamn it, there is nothing to remember!" Conklin said. He was still enjoying his angry mood. "That Chambrun clown seems to expect us to come up with magic tricks for him."

"He's not a stupid man," I said.

"What could we possibly have forgotten that would help him?" Conklin asked. "I don't know who Geoff Hammond invited for breakfast. He didn't tell me. He didn't tell Bobby. No reason why he should have. We each had our jobs to do, which didn't involve his breakfast. If he wanted to invite a friend, he didn't have to ask our permission, for God sake, or tell us about it."

"So who were his friends?" I asked. "Particularly one who was friendly enough to strangle him to death?"

Bobby Bryan gave me a wry little smile. "A question

Roy and I have just been asking ourselves," he said. "I told you a little about Geoff the other day, Mark. Wheeling and dealing with people who wheel and deal for money and power. It doesn't have to have been a friend in the true sense of that word. Geoff didn't have close friends who he'd just invite in casually for an early morning breakfast. It wasn't a social time of day for him. You can depend on it's being business, and I don't mean the kind of business Roy handled for him. Nothing to do with television or lecture dates. Some kind of secret shenanigans that Roy and I were never in on. He was putting the screws on someone, and that someone fought back. That's my theory, and I think Roy buys it, too."

"It could have been anyone, from anyplace in the world," Conklin said. He gave me a nasty look. "I hardly dare suggest to a friend of Chambrun's that it could have been some kind of Zionist terror boy."

"Or Arab terror boy, or South African terror boy," Bobby said. "Brown, or black, or—green. The color of money." He shook his head. "Where we draw a complete blank, Mark, is any possible connection with Joanna Fraser."

"Which is what takes Chambrun back to High Crest two years ago," I said. "Joanna Fraser was there. Ziegler, the dead private eye, was there."

"But we weren't!" Conklin said. "Not me, not Bobby, not Hammond. Weren't there then, never have been there. None of us knew Joanna Fraser or had any contact with her. How the hell could we possibly guess who she was having a martini with? And I hope it was better than this one." He emptied his glass and put it down, hard, on the table.

I stood up. "Keep concentrating on your terror boy, whatever nationality or color," I said. "Maybe we can make a connection between him and Joanna Fraser that you'd have no way of knowing about." I turned to go. "One thing I think you ought to keep in mind, Conklin,"

I said to the angry one. "Chambrun is far from being an amateur at dealing with violence. Try cooperating with him. It might just help to keep one of us from being the killer's next target."

One of the things that tends to happen to you in the middle of a murder case like this is grabbing at straws that don't have any real substance. I had come up with one. Bobby Bryan had made sense to me. Hammond could have breakfasted with someone involved in his secret power playing. Zionist, Arab, South African, Bobby had suggested. The Middle East had been Hammond's playground. If that notion held together, then it would make sense to find out if Joanna Fraser had any dealings with that part of the world. Either Nora Coyle or Colin Dobler could have answers to that. Dobler had probably gone back to his own quarters or to Gramercy Park, but I thought I knew where to find Nora.

She was in my apartment, having coffee with the young cop who was assigned to guard her.

"It really isn't fair for me to camp out here," she said.

"It's fine with me," I said. I thought there was a faint heightening of color in her cheeks. She was undoubtedly remembering that we had shared my bed last night. I wondered if she was thinking I'd been a nice guy for not taking advantage of her—or some kind of village idiot for missing my chance.

I didn't want to talk to her about my idea in the presence of the cop. He wasn't a detective on the case, just someone assigned to keep anyone from coming up behind Nora unexpectedly.

"Time for a drink," I said, and guided Nora out into the kitchenette. While I broke out ice, I told her I had some questions for her.

"I've been racking my brains, Mark," she said. "I can think of a hundred women who might have dropped in for a drink with Joanna that day. But men?"

"I had a feeling you might be protecting Dobler when you couldn't remember any men," I said.

"I like Colin," she said. "I think he was rather badly treated by Joanna. He loved her, so he took what she dished out without ever complaining—that I heard. But if I knew of any man I'd have told Mr. Chambrun."

"But there must have been men, not necessarily lovers," I said. I asked her what she'd like to drink. She didn't want anything and, as a matter of fact, neither did I. I poured some soda into two glasses, added a twist of lemon, and we sat at the kitchenette table, staring at each other. It was as if we were trying to force something sensible to emerge from one of us.

"Joanna was a very gregarious person," Nora said, groping for that sensible something. "She liked people, all kinds of people. She enjoyed being with them, talking to them about anything that interested them. Men as well as women."

"You mean," I said, grinning at her, "that she was willing to admit that men are people?"

"She wasn't a nut, Mark," Nora said. "She went along, in public, with a lot of clichés that the 'new woman' makes about men, and the discrimination against women in modern society. But in private she laughed at a lot of it and at a lot of the women who've pushed themselves forward as spokesmen—spokeswomen—for women's causes."

"Think about men, luv," I said. "We're concerned about men. It wasn't a woman who sneaked up behind Mrs. Fraser with a roll of picture wire."

A little shudder ran over her slim body. Joanna had not only been her employer but her friend.

"There are three or four men who work on her magazine *Liberation* in the business, circulation, and advertising end," she said.

"Isn't that a contradiction?"

"She was a very sound business woman," Nora said.

"She'd been asked that question. She always said those men would be replaced by women when women learned the jobs. But she wouldn't allow crucial positions to be held except by the most competent people she could find. The 'cause' wasn't enough to justify anything but the best."

"Any of those men could have dropped by and she'd have invited them up for a drink?"

"Of course. They were close working associates."

"Hardy should be given a list of them," I said. "It should be part of his methodical checkout."

"No problem," Nora said. "They were all in touch that first day, shocked and concerned."

I fiddled with my glass of soda, not really wanting it. "You and Joanna traveled a lot?" I asked.

"All over Europe. Joanna lectured in most of the big cities where there are women's movements. London, Paris, Brussels, West Berlin, a women's congress in Geneva, Switzerland, Rome. So many places."

"The Middle East?"

She gave me a nostalgic little laugh. "The Middle East was a project for the next decade," she said. "Women there are really kept under wraps by their men. The men, Joanna used to say, are almost paranoid about keeping their women as sex objects. How could we persuade them to set their women free when we haven't managed the simplest kind of equal rights for our own women, in a free world?"

"She have contacts with people there?" I asked.

"Not that I know of. She tried to arrange a meeting with President Sadat of Egypt on one of his visits here, but he smelled it out as a publicity gimmick—which it was—and regretted that he couldn't fit a meeting into his busy schedule."

Then I explained to her why I was asking about the Middle East. It was Hammond's special interest. He undoubtedly had enemies there. His breakfast guest could

147

have been someone from there. I was looking for some connection between that possible breakfast guest and Joanna.

Nora shook her head. "It just doesn't fit in with anything I know about her, Mark."

So much for that particular straw.

My telephone began to ring and I picked up the extension, which was a wall-set in the kitchenette. It was Betsy Ruysdale.

"Alvin Parker has come up with something he thinks Chambrun or Hardy ought to know, but I can't locate either of them."

I told her where Hardy was.

"Not now he isn't," Ruysdale said. "Both he and Chambrun have left the hotel."

"Left?" For Chambrun to leave the Beaumont was an event.

"They've gone to talk to Guido Maroni's wife," she said. "The missing waiter. I suggested to Parker that he talk to you."

"Where is he?"

"In his suite on the twelfth floor. Twelve nineteen. Shall I call him and tell him you're on your way? After all, you're our expert listener."

"Hear everything, understand nothing," I said. "Sure, call him."

I went along the corridor to the elevators. I suddenly had the uncomfortable feeling that someone might be watching me. My own private paranoia, I thought.

The neat little executive director of the Parker Foundation was waiting for me in 1219. He was dressed as if he was going to a formal luncheon. I guessed he was never caught with his image down.

"It's hard to believe," he said, "but I've remembered something about two years ago that nobody else seems to have mentioned.

"At High Crest?"

148

"Of course—yes. I had forgotten it in all of the—the horror here. But it seems strange to me that Miss Coyle, or Mr. Dobler, or some of the people at High Crest haven't mentioned it. Of course, maybe they have and nobody has bothered to mention it to me."

"I can't answer that unless you tell me what it is," I said.

He took a neatly folded handkerchief out of his pocket and blotted at the little beads of sweat on his upper lip and his forehead. He seemed to have trouble breathing.

"Has nobody mentioned that the night Hal Carpenter was murdered Joanna Fraser saw someone outside his cabin?" he asked.

I just stared at him. Surer than hell nobody had mentioned such a thing in my hearing. I could feel the hackles rising on the back of my neck.

"It wasn't a secret at the time," Parker said. "She went to the police with it. Why it hasn't been brought up I can't imagine."

"Why you've only just remembered it is on the odd side," I said.

He shook his head from side to side like a man suffering from guilt. "There was so much else—one thing after another. I had the Foundation ball on my mind, everyone frightened, almost hysterical. But after I left Mr. Chambrun's office this morning I suddenly realized that nobody had mentioned what seemed to me to be an important fact."

"So two years later this person she saw kills her and two other people?"

"I don't know. But doesn't it seem to you—?"

"Yes, it does," I said. "You say she went to the police?"

"Yes. She couldn't describe the person she saw, except that it was a man. The police weren't, I think, particularly interested. They were already convinced about Sharon Dain. There were over three hundred guests at High Crest. There wasn't anything unusual about someone wandering around the cabin area, even late at night. Ms.

Fraser was asked to keep an eye open—a hundred and fifty male guests at least—for someone she might recognize. She said, from the beginning, that she wouldn't know him if she came face to face with him. She was trying to make the point—she told me—that there was someone else hanging around Carpenter's cabin the night of the murder. The police should know that, should look for someone else besides Sharon Dain."

"She told you?"

"I—I was heading up the defense committee for Sharon Dain," Parker said. "She came to me with five hundred dollars. She was angry because the police had brushed what she had to tell them under the rug. I think that's why she contributed. It never came up again, you know—all through the trial. Max Steiner must have felt it wasn't worth using."

The thought I had was too farfetched to make sense. Two years ago Joanna Fraser sees someone hanging around Carpenter's cabin the night of his murder. It's night. She can't identify him. Just someone. Then, two years later, in the Beaumont, she suddenly can identify him, lets him know that, and he wraps a strand of wire around her neck. Far out, and yet I couldn't shake it.

I used Parker's phone to call Max Steiner. He was in court, or out to lunch, or something. His office simply said he was not there and they couldn't say when he was expected. I left a message for him to call me back, and then I got the switchboard to put through a person-to-person call to Jack Galt at High Crest. It would be about eleven o'clock in the morning out there. I got lucky.

"What's new?" Galt asked me.

I told him we were still floundering, but why hadn't he told me that Joanna Fraser had seen someone the night of Carpenter's murder?

"It was a nothing," he said.

"Some nothing! She's dead and it just might tie in."

"Look, Mark, I chased that down from top to bottom at

150

the time," the detective said. "Along with other similar leads. A dozen people thought they saw someone wandering around that night. And there *were* people, going from one cabin to another. Some of them were identified, came forward, told us what they were doing. It checked out. Whoever it was Joanna Fraser saw, it could have been one of those. I got a police artist to try to draw a picture of the man she said she saw. She didn't have anything to offer; no face, nothing outstanding like very tall, or very short. Nothing for the artist to even start a mock-up. The police wrote it off. I wrote it off. She saw someone, and there were people around, but what she had was valueless."

"Max Steiner didn't buy it either?"

"There wasn't anything to use," Galt said. "He knew that people had been wandering around in the cabin area, but someone who couldn't be identified, couldn't be described, wasn't of any value, even if he was seen by an important lady."

"If she couldn't describe him then, it doesn't seem likely she would suddenly recognize him two years later," I said.

"I'd say no way," Galt said. "Steiner did use the fact that other people had been seen in the cabin area, but he didn't mention that Joanna Fraser had seen someone because it was just an echo of what other people—with more details—had seen. I didn't mention it to you because I'd long ago erased it from my mind as having any bearing on the case."

"Even though she'd just been strangled by the same guy who killed out there, the guy she may have seen?"

"Mark, it's a meaningless coincidence. Remember something. Nobody who was at High Crest the night Carpenter was murdered was allowed to leave. Not for three days. Joanna Fraser had three days in which to circulate, to look for her night prowler. In fact, the police urged her to do just that. She came up empty. It was such a thoroughly useless fact that I just plain forgot about it."

I couldn't let it go. "Who says the person who murdered Carpenter was a guest at High Crest?" I asked. "Who says he had to be hanging around for three days to be identified by someone? Who says he couldn't have come in off the road after dark, knocked off his man, and taken a powder? Al Ziegler's mysterious client who even Ziegler couldn't identify?"

"You don't know that for a fact—about Ziegler's client," Galt said. I thought he sounded just a little hooked. "That's something dreamed up back there in Chambrun country."

"It's as good as anything we have to go on," I said.

"I can dig up the police record on what Joanna said she saw," Galt said. "As I remember she said she saw a man, his back turned to her, looking in Carpenter's window. I don't think it's any more than that. Surely the Coyle girl or her husband would remember what Joanna Fraser had to say about it at that time."

"You're one step ahead of me," I said. "But don't you wonder why neither of them has thought it worth mentioning up to now?"

"Same reason I didn't," Galt said. "It was a nothing then, and I'm afraid you're going to find it's a nothing now."

Parker seemed relieved to hear that other people had failed to remember the incident. I guess it made him feel less guilty. I headed back down to the second floor and Nora.

She looked at me, wide eyed, when I laid it on the line for her. "But of course!" she said.

"Of course what? Of course it wasn't worth mentioning?"

"It was two years ago, Mark!"

"But everything connected with that time must have seemed important after she was killed the same way Carpenter was," I said. "She must have talked to you about it. She must have talked to Dobler about it. Neither of you thought it was worth mentioning?"

"I don't know about Colin," she said. "But I swear I just didn't think about it. It turned out to have no importance at the time. I've been asked so many questions about so many other things the last two days."

I thought she was near to tears.

"Tell me everything about what Joanna saw and thought back there at High Crest." I guided her over to the couch and sat beside her, my arm around her shoulders. To hell with the cop who sat stolidly on the chair by the front door.

"Two of the women in Joanna's liberation group had one of the cabins there at High Crest," Nora said. "Joanna went to visit with them that night. I don't remember any particular reason why. Maybe just to have a drink and socialize. The cabin where her friends were was a couple of hundred yards from the main building where she and I were housed. Sometime after midnight she walked back. I was already in bed and she didn't disturb me. I could hear her moving around in the next room. It wasn't too easy to sleep. The piano was still going strong in the main hall, people singing." I could feel Nora's body shudder. "Then there was this crazy screaming outside somewhere. I could hear people running out to whoever was making the commotion. It was Sharon Dain, but we didn't know that till later. You remember her story? She'd been knocked unconscious. When she came to she'd found Carpenter, strangled with picture wire.

"Well, we couldn't go calmly to sleep with all that clamor outside. Joanna and I both got dressed and joined other people in the big room. That's when we heard what it was, everybody talking at once. The police came in about fifteen minutes. Mike Chandler was trying to keep everyone away from where it had happened."

"And Joanna told them she'd seen somebody at the cabin?"

"Not then. She didn't mention anything about it then."

"Why?"

"Because I don't think she realized she'd seen anything then. It wasn't until the next morning. Everybody went to gawk at the cabin where it had happened. You know, there were state police, photographers, God knows who else. When we saw which cabin it was, Joanna grabbed my arm and said, 'Would you believe I saw someone peering in the window of that place on my way home last night?' That's when she went to the state police."

"She hadn't mentioned it to you the night before?"

"No reason to, before we heard the screaming. No reason to afterward until she saw what cabin it was where Carpenter and Sharon Dain were living. She didn't connect the two things until they connected themselves—if you see what I mean."

"How did she describe what she saw?"

"She said a man was standing close to the window, arms spread out as though he was holding onto the window frame, his back to her. She stood watching him for a moment, and then he walked away, around the corner of the cabin toward the front door. That was all. She never saw his face."

"It was dark?"

"There was moonlight, but he never turned her way."

"And the troopers thought that wasn't worth following up?"

"They were pretty cynical about it, Mark. And other people had seen people wandering around. It wasn't any secret that Carpenter was always playing sex games with some woman or other. A Peeping Tom they said of Joanna's man, trying to get a look at what was cooking inside. They'd already decided that Sharon Dain was it."

"Joanna was angry about it?"

"No. She shrugged it off. She'd done her duty, told what she'd seen. As the gossip got really loud I think she decided the police were probably right—she'd seen a Peeping Tom."

"Alvin Parker says she was angry about it when she gave him money for the defense fund."

"She wasn't angry about her story being ignored," Nora said, "but she was contemptuous of the police. She felt they'd settled on Sharon Dain without looking anywhere else. 'Typical male chauvinist pigs,' she called them." Nora laughed. "A common phrase in the liberation movement. Mr. Parker probably mistook it for anger."

"You must have talked about it afterward," I said. "No description of the man she saw that stood out at all?"

"Mark, it was January," she said. "Bitter cold, probably below zero. Everybody at High Crest wore the same kind of clothing—ski pants, boots, parkas with hoods to keep your ears from freezing. Your face would be hidden unless you were looking straight at someone. That kind of winter protection was almost like a uniform out there."

Like the cowboy regalia they were wearing out there now, in summer, I thought.

"Joanna must have tried hard to remember something distinctive about the man she saw."

"I don't know what you mean by 'tried hard,' Mark. The police asked her. She told them what she'd seen—a man, bundled up, parka hood over his head, standing with his face right against Carpenter's window. There wasn't anything else to remember, so she wasn't trying hard." Nora twisted in my arm and looked up at me. "At the time, Mark, it had just happened! She didn't have to dredge something up out of the past, something she might have forgotten. It was all right then, a fresh experience."

"Did she talk about it often afterward? After you'd left High Crest?"

"I don't think so, Mark. I mean, not about that man. We followed the Sharon Dain case in the papers and on TV. Joanna still thought she'd been railroaded by a gang of insensitive males. But I don't remember her talking about the man she saw. He hadn't proved out. I'm telling you the truth, Mark, when I say I hadn't thought about him for

155

a long time, almost two years, until you reminded me of him just now."

"Not even when you found her, killed the way Carpenter was killed?"

"You don't believe me, do you?" she said. "Perhaps there's no way to make you understand. I—I went shopping for Joanna that morning, personal things, hair shampoo, some—some coloring she used. A book she wanted at Brentano's. I came back and I—I found her." Her whole body began to tremble again. "Do you think I stood there, wondering if she'd been killed by a man she saw looking in a window two years ago, in a place two thousand miles away? I didn't think of anything but getting help! Damn it, Mark, I was in shock! Your Mr. Dodd came, and then the police. All the questions then and later have centered on who might have joined her for cocktails, who her friends were, who her enemies were, if any. Do you imagine it popped into my head that she might have made drinks for a man she didn't know, couldn't identify, certainly hadn't thought of for months and months and months? Of course it didn't. That man hadn't crossed my mind for almost two years and he didn't then. I didn't even think about it and reject it. Can you understand that?"

I supposed I had to. It made sense. And yet—"Now that I've reminded you?" I said.

"Nothing makes any sense, Mark!" And the tears came. "If that man she saw is the killer, she couldn't have done him any harm. She wouldn't have known him from Adam! You've got a policeman guarding me, but what possible danger could I be to him? I never even saw him at High Crest—with his back turned! Joanna may have talked to Colin about the man she saw, two years ago, but Colin never saw him, was never even at High Crest. Colin couldn't harm that man, but you're guarding him, too. Either one of us could sit down and have a drink with that man and not have the faintest idea that he was Joanna's

156

Peeping Tom. Don't you see, it just doesn't add up, Mark."

It didn't, but, somehow, I didn't want to drop it. At least, I thought, I must present my notion to Chambrun and Hardy and let them reject it. There was no way I could foresee that it would be quite some time before I would get to that.

I tried to soothe Nora's tattered nerves and then went out into the hall to head for Chambrun's office. I came face to face with Chambrun outside my door. He'd just come off the elevator and was walking briskly, head down, toward his quarters. I was shocked when he looked at me. This was the hanging judge, his face a white marble mask. For a moment I thought he didn't recognize me.

"We found Guido Maroni," he said in a flat, cold voice.

"Good," I said.

"In a trash barrel in the basement of his house," Chambrun said. "Picture wire."

He brushed past me and went on down the hall.

CHAPTER FOUR

There is no way I could have been everyplace at once. When I came to writing down an account of this grim and bizarre adventure there were key parts of it to which I couldn't be a witness. One of them was the discovery of Guido Maroni. In a calmer aftermath I did get the details of those events from Chambrun and Hardy and Jerry Dodd, our security chief.

As I have reported, Hardy sent Sergeant Baxter to look for Guido and talk to his wife, Sarafina. Baxter was still working on the theory that Guido had gone out to buy a paper, run into some friends, been lionized for his role in the Hammond murder, and got himself potted. The trail faded out for Baxter after a while. He located the news-stand where Guido had bought a copy of the *Post*. Mrs. Maroni had indicated where Guido might go to buy his paper. She'd also told Baxter of a local pub where Guido and his friends were in the habit of gathering. She'd even given Baxter the names of several of Guido's chums.

The newsdealer remembered Guido's buying the paper. They'd talked for a minute or two about the murders at the Beaumont, which had made the headlines. Guido, the newsdealer reported, seemed to be in a highly nervous state. He could have gone to the pub that Sarafina Maroni had mentioned. Guido would have had to pass it on the way home, so the direction Guido took, with his newspaper tucked under his arm, didn't provide an answer.

The proprietor of the pub was quite definite, however. Guido had not stopped there. The proprietor and some of Guido's pals had hoped that he would, eager to hear the real dirt from the horse's mouth. But Guido hadn't ever come, not that night, nor the next day, nor today.

When Baxter went back to Sarafina Maroni, she went into hysterics. Baxter was swamped under a torrent of words, spoken in Italian, not one of which he understood. It was clear that she was convinced of disaster. Her wailings and moanings suggested she was already mourning her missing husband.

Baxter got in touch with Hardy. He needed a cop who could speak Italian. It happened that Hardy was in Chambrun's office when the call came from the sergeant. He had taken Dick Barrows, the *Times* man, there to discuss just how much special consideration they would give him. He relayed Baxter's call to them.

"I'll go with you," Chambrun said. "I know Mrs. Maroni and I speak Italian. She will trust me."

Chambrun knows the people who work for him well, makes a point of it. Twice a year there was a huge party

158

for the staff and their families. Chambrun knew what the status of all the marriages was, how many kids they had, the states of their health. He dealt compassionately with their problems. His door was open to them and they counted on him. That was the reason loyalty to him was so intense among his people.

Chambrun and Hardy and Dick Barrows went to the Maroni apartment on the Upper East Side. Sarafina Maroni was in a pitiable state. She took one look at Chambrun and clung to him for dear life. He held her, stroking her oily black hair, soothing her in her own language.

It came out of her in bits and pieces. Guido knew something he hadn't told the police. Something about a man who bumped into his wagon when he was delivering breakfast to Hammond's suite. At the time it hadn't seemed important, but when he got home and thought about it, he decided it was something Mr. Chambrun should know.

"He would have come to you the next morning when he returned to work," Sarafina said. Oceans of tears. "But he never came home from buying his paper."

"He thought the man who bumped into his wagon might be important to me?" Chambrun asked.

"Si, si!" Vigorous noddings. "He thought the man who bumped into his wagon might be the one for whom the second breakfast on the wagon was intended."

"Did Guido describe this man, Sarafina?"

Guido had not. It would not have been important to his wife. "But he would have described him to you!"

The newsstand where Guido had bought his paper was only a block away. According to the newsdealer, Guido had headed for his home after buying his copy of the *Post*. That was about six o'clock in the evening, broad daylight.

"Have Baxter search the alleys between here and the newsstand," Chambrun said to Hardy. "And then this house, from top to bottom."

In less than an hour, while I was playing games with

Parker and Nora, Baxter had found Guido's body in the basement of the house, jammed into a metal trash can, strangled with picture wire.

Another of Hardy's tortuous routines was underway, with cops questioning all the tenants in the Maronis's building, storekeepers in the neighborhood, children who had been playing on the street. Who had seen what around suppertime the day before yesterday? With luck, in that kind of tenement area, someone might remember a stranger, a man out of place. Dick Barrows was working with the cops, trying to dig out his own story for the *Times*.

I had followed Chambrun into his office after our encounter in the hall outside my place. He walked past Betsy Ruysdale in her outer room without a word. She and I followed him.

He sat down behind his desk, rigid, not looking at either of us, his face still that pale marble mask. Then he raised his right fist and brought it down on the desk so hard that everything on it jumped.

"I blame myself!" he said in a bitter voice.

Ruysdale didn't have a clue to what he was talking about. I whispered to her the news about Guido. He told us then, briefly, what I have just outlined about his visit to Sarafina Maroni and the grim discovery in the tenement basement.

"I should have insisted on being present when the staff was questioned," he said. "But we were faced with panic here in the hotel."

"What difference would it have made?" I asked.

"Guido Maroni would have kept his cool if I'd been there," Chambrun said. "He trusted me. Like most people of his kind, cops were the enemy to him. He answered what they asked him, offered nothing of his own. Perhaps he hadn't thought it through. I don't even know what they asked him, for God sake! My first question would have been had he seen anyone who might have been the breakfast guest?"

"Surely Hardy or Baxter—" I began.

"Nothing is sure unless you are there yourself," Chambrun said. "Guido undoubtedly had a bad case of hysterics. He'd found the body, eyes popping out, tongue protruding. All he wanted to do was get out of there, get away, get home." He turned to Ruysdale. "Get Jerry Dodd here as fast as you can. Call Ray Dominic and get him here, too." Dominic is the headwaiter in charge of room service. Ruysdale took off for her own phone.

Chambrun had pulled a yellow pad toward him and was making notes on it in great bold strokes. "It was eight o'clock when Guido arrived on the thirty-fourth floor with Hammond's breakfast. He bumped into a stranger in the hallway. In view of what's happened we have to think that was the killer." He drew an angry line under what he had written. "We don't know the exact time Hammond was killed, but it was before ten o'clock, which was when Guido found him. Two hours later Joanna Fraser was making martinis for that same killer. Nora Coyle found her dead at about one o'clock. Within the space of five hours, eight to one o'clock, our man has managed two murders. No fingerprints, no trace of anything to lead to him. A careful man. But there was one thing he couldn't have prepared for."

"Bumping into Guido?"

"Right!" Another savage line across the pad. "Guido might have mentioned it, might even have described him. But until Guido could actually point a finger at him he was safe. What should the next question be, Mark?"

"How did he find Guido?" I suggested.

"Good man," Chambrun said. "He wouldn't know Guido's name, unless he's a guest in the hotel who may have been served by Guido. The man has certainly been practically living in the Beaumont the last three days, whether or not he has a room here. But knowing Guido's name wouldn't lead him to the tenement where Guido lived. He had to ask someone."

"Who would give it to him?"

"Some plausible story might pry it out of someone," Chambrun said. "Something that looked like doing a favor for Guido. We have rules about giving out addresses, but rules are made to be broken. However he got the address, he got it. He is hanging around Guido's tenement when Guido goes out to buy his paper, follows him back to the house, and attacks him in a dark hallway. From behind, as usual. Drags the body down to the basement and stuffs it in a barrel."

Another line slashed across the page.

"He's safe then," Chambrun said, "to stay around the hotel."

"Why isn't he long gone?" I asked.

"A guess," Chambrun said. "He couldn't leave because he would be missed. Because leaving would attract attention to him."

"Someone on our staff?"

"I'd bet against it," Chambrun said. "If you want to follow that line, Mark, get me a list of our people who spent the skiing season at High Crest two years ago. The man we're looking for was there. No, Mark, he's not one of ours."

"So he stays in the hotel, sees Ziegler-Davis wandering around, and knows he's in trouble again," I said. "Ziegler could identify him."

"On the contrary, if we're right he couldn't. Ziegler hadn't any idea what he looked like."

"So why didn't he just ignore Ziegler?"

"Ask him when we catch up with him," Chambrun said. "Because I promise you we will, Mark. Guido was my friend and employee, the others were my guests. If I don't get him, I wouldn't have the gall to sit in this chair any longer."

Jerry Dodd and Raimondo Dominic, an elegant headwaiter type, came in together, followed by Miss Ruysdale. Chambrun told them what had happened to Guido.

Jerry reacted with a kind of tight-lipped anger. He was responsible for security in the hotel and he had to feel that someone was making him look like an incompetent fool. Dominic looked shocked. Guido had been one of his crew.

"It's hard to believe," he said.

"Believe," Chambrun said grimly. "I saw the poor bastard stuffed in a garbage can. But you see where we're at, both of you? Guido had an encounter with the killer just before he served Hammond his breakfast. Any gossip in your section, Ray?"

"About that? No." Dominic shook his head. "I took the order for breakfast from thirty-four-oh-six myself. Juice, eggs and bacon, toast and coffee for two. On the phone the man said he was 'Mr. Conklin.' I learned later that Hammond was registered under that name."

"He was," Chambrun said. "A 'John Smith'—with our knowledge."

"He asked to be served promptly at eight o'clock," Dominic said. "I'd have to look at the slip, but I guess his call came about twenty minutes past seven. Thirty-four and thirty-five were the floors Guido was assigned to. It was routine for him to deliver the order to thirty-four-oh-six."

"When he came back from making that delivery, did he have anything to say?" Chambrun asked. "Bumping into someone or being bumped into?"

"No," Dominic said. "I saw him when he came back. He was in a lather. Eight o'clock is our busiest time. Everybody wants breakfast at the same moment. Guido had other orders to deliver. He just went about his business." Dominic gave Chambrun a sad little smile. "He always talked to himself a mile a minute in Italian when he was rushed. But it was just his usual complaint that God put too many burdens on his shoulders. Afterward—" and Dominic raised his hands in a helpless gesture.

"Afterward?"

"When he went to get the wagon in thirty-four-oh-six and found the body," Dominic said. "Then he was overcome with—with horror, would you say? Jabbering away like a crazy man. Jerry, who was the first to question him, can tell you. He was like demented."

Jerry nodded. "I don't speak Italian either. I had a time getting him to say something I could understand."

"He reported to you what he'd found?"

"No. No, he ran down the hall to the housekeeper's room. You remember, boss, it was Mrs. Kniffin who reported to us. She managed to keep Guido there till I got to him. He didn't really have a story to tell, you know. He took the breakfast wagon to thirty-four-oh-six, Hammond told him where to place it, and he left. He didn't see who the breakfast guest was. He went back at ten o'clock and found—what he found." Jerry shrugged. "After Sergeant Baxter got that out of him, I told Guido to go home and get himself pulled together. Not to bother to come in till the next day."

Chambrun glanced at his pad. "So how did the killer get Guido's address?"

Jerry and Dominic looked at each other.

"I gave his address to the police," Dominic said, "but certainly not to anyone else."

Chambrun's eyes narrowed as he turned to Jerry. "You say Sergeant Baxter questioned Guido?"

"Yeah, before Guido went home. Baxter agreed there was no use his staying around. He really had nothing to tell that would help the cops."

"Tell me, Jerry," Chambrun said very quietly, "what is the first question the police ask when they are questioning a witness?"

"Name and address," Jerry said. His eyes widened. "Oh, brother!"

Chambrun looked at Dominic. "So how did you come to give Guido's address to the police?"

Dominic looked confused for a moment. "Why, I was at

my station in room service. The phone rang and a man said he was Sergeant Somebody. He wanted the name and address of the waiter who'd found the body in thirty-four-oh-six. It was the police, so I gave it to him."

"Like hell it was the police!" Chambrun said.

"The whole place was a madhouse," Dominic said. "I never thought—"

"I suppose there's no reason why you should have," Chambrun said. He sounded tired. He'd said there'd be an easy way for the killer to get the address, a plausible story. What could be more plausible than a police request to a distracted member of the staff?

"My God!" Dominic said. "I helped to get him killed!"

"I think the killer would have found a way without you, Ray," Chambrun said. "Don't blame yourself." He straightened up in his chair. "This is what I want you to do, both of you. Find out everyone Guido talked to from the time he delivered breakfast to thirty-four-oh-six until he was sent home after he discovered the murder. There's a chance he may have told someone about the man who bumped into him in the hallway. It's the only lead we've got."

"Not much of a lead," Jerry said.

"Good enough for someone to kill Guido to hide it," Chambrun said.

I told Chambrun what had been bugging me before the news about the unfortunate Guido had broken. He listened to my account of what Joanna Fraser had seen two years ago at High Crest and how everyone had conveniently forgotten it until Alvin Parker found it lurking somewhere in his conscience. Chambrun listened, squinting at me through the smoke from his cigarette.

"Describe Paul Newman to me," he said, when I had finished.

Games, yet! So I described Paul Newman as I recalled

him: six feet tall, or a little more, blond, blue eyes, good athletic build.

"But if there wasn't a label on that description—a name attached to it—it could fit a thousand men," Chambrun said.

"Well, I don't know about his warts or his birthmarks," I said.

"Not important," Chambrun said. "Let's look at it for a moment, Mark. Hammond knew who he was, invited him for breakfast. He killed Hammond because Hammond had something on him. That's the assumption, right? But he killed Joanna Fraser, you're saying, because she suddenly recognized him. How? All she saw at High Crest was a man, his back to her, bundled up in winter clothes with a parka over his head. That could have been Paul Newman and she'd have no idea of it. She could have come face to face with Paul Newman, or Robert Redford, or Jesus Christ in the lobby and she'd have no reason to connect any one of them with the backside of a man in winter clothes with a parka over his head."

"So she wasn't killed because she suddenly recognized him after two years," I said. "He wasn't dressed for winter skiing in the Beaumont lobby in June!"

"Let's not reject that idea entirely, but let's move on," Chambrun said. "No question about the motive for killing poor Guido. He collided with the killer in the hall outside thirty-four-oh-six. He could have described that man in a way that would have left no doubts about him. Bobby Bryan or Roy Conklin would have recognized that description as someone with whom Hammond had dealings. What could Guido have told us except that the man was a certain height, a certain coloring, a certain build? A general description, like your description of Paul Newman."

"Most likely he would have told us he was a guest he'd served in a certain room. That would identify him for us," I said.

166

"Could be," Chambrun said. "But how would that have meant anything to Joanna Fraser?"

I gave up. "Maybe he had two heads," I said.

Chambrun gave me a steady look. "Perhaps that's closer than you know, Mark," he said. "Joanna Fraser would have noticed that from behind, wouldn't she? Two heads, two parkas."

"Oh, come on, boss!" I said.

"I haven't suggested a scar on his face, or that he was 'brown, or black, or green' as young Bryan suggested to you, because Joanna Fraser didn't see his face at High Crest. But two heads? Quite a remarkable idea, my friend."

So if he wanted to kid around that was up to him. He suggested that I join Jerry in hunting for someone to whom Guido might have spoken about his collision on the thirty-fourth floor. I decided he wanted to be rid of me and my wisecracks. Hell, you get so twisted up in a thing like this that you decide to say something funny or cut your throat.

I went down to the lobby to look for Johnny Thacker, the day bell captain. He's a smart cookie who's worked in the Beaumont for fifteen years, sees all, knows all. He can tell you what old man is enjoying himself in what wrong room with what young woman. He could have made a million bucks if he'd decided to turn to blackmail as a profession. He was enormously valuable to Chambrun because he chose to turn anything he knew over to the head man. Staff people trusted Johnny, passed along their own bits of gossip to him. I figured if he was turned loose on the Guido business he was the most likely person to hear something.

I briefed Johnny.

"If Guido said anything to anyone I'll come up with it," he said. "Tell the boss I'm taking myself off duty for a while. Joe Nemjou can take over for me."

I turned away and came face to face with Colin Dobler,

who was crossing the lobby toward the elevators. Just behind him, like a dutiful St. Bernard dog, was the bodyguard assigned to him.

"I hoped the police would let me get into Joanna's apartment," Dobler said. "Believe it or not, I'm the executor of her estate. All her papers are up there. There may be things that need immediate handling."

"Get your shadow here to ask Hardy's permission. He's in the executive room across the lobby there," I said. "I'll buy you a drink in the Spartan Bar. There's something I'd like to ask you."

The Spartan Bar is one of the last strictly male bastions in the city. Oh, we don't admit that women are not welcome there. But they are not allowed in "unescorted," and anyone who brings a lady is likely to find all the tables reserved the next time he appears. It is really a hangout for older men, almost like a club, where they play chess, and backgammon, and gin rummy, and talk about how great they were at whatever they did thirty years ago.

Dobler gave me a sad little smile as I took him to a table.

"This was one of Joanna's targets," he said. "It was unthinkable that there should be a men-only bar in the place where she lived. But Chambrun and the maitre d' here were too smart for her. It's a saga in itself. She was a good enough sport to be amused at the way they maneuvered her."

I ordered drinks and told him what was on my mind. How come he hadn't mentioned that Joanna had seen someone outside Carpenter's cabin at High Crest the night of the murder, two years ago?

He gave me pretty much the same answer Nora had. Of course he wasn't there. But later, when Joanna came back and they were together, she'd told him about seeing someone, but that the police hadn't been interested.

"Her description of the man she saw?" I asked.

"There wasn't exactly a description, as I remember,"

168

Dobler said. "His back was to her, bundled up in winter gear. I know she said she couldn't possibly have identified him. Never saw his face."

"Did she—how shall I put it—brood over the fact that the police ignored what she'd seen?"

"Men!" he said, with a little laugh. "You can't expect anything very intelligent from men. I don't remember her ever talking about it after she first came back. It wasn't as if she could have testified to something under oath."

"So how could she have recognized this man two years later, invited him for drinks, left herself open to attack?"

Dobler looked at me as though I wasn't quite bright.

"That's what we think," I said. "That, somehow, Joanna spotted this man, which is why he killed her. But why invite him for drinks?"

"She couldn't have spotted him," Dobler said. "She never saw his face. He was just a bundle of clothes with his back turned. She didn't have a notion, from what she saw, whether he was young or old." He shook his head slowly. "Joanna was a mass of contradictions," he said slowly. "She headed a crusade for women—against men. Yet she admired certain traditional male attributes. She wanted to be a 'gentleman,' a 'sportsman,' play the game by the rules." He shook his head slowly, from side to side. "If she saw this man—and I say it's possible—and something about him made her wonder, but she was uncertain—she might have decided that the sportsmanlike thing to do was to confront him with it before she blew the whistle on him. But I swear to you, Haskell, she never mentioned anything that would make me believe there was anything that would lead her to suspect someone."

"He didn't have two heads?"

Dobler laughed. "She never mentioned it if he did."

Johnny Thacker came hurrying into the Spartan. He excused himself to Dobler. "I haven't found anyone who talked to Guido," Johnny told me, "but Carl Brewer, the operator on elevator four in the main bank, saw it happen."

"Saw what happen?"

"The collision Guido had with someone in the hallway on thirty-four. I'm taking him up to the boss. Thought you'd like to know."

Carl Brewer's was a face I'd seen every morning of my life since I'd come to work at the Beaumont. He is what we call a "B and S" behind Chambrun's back—B and S for Bright and Shining. The first faces a guest sees in the morning should be smiling and happy, not hung over like the guest himself might be. I remember arguing about it with Chambrun. There were mornings in my life when if anyone gave me that good-cheer routine I'd have kicked him right in his Pepsodent smile.

"The largest percentage of people," Chambrun told me, "don't have your jaundiced view of life."

"Only some mornings," I said.

That afternoon Johnny Thacker had encountered Carl Brewer just as he was coming off his shift. The news about Guido had already spread backstage like a forest fire. Johnny saw that if he didn't ask about Guido, people would tell him. Carl Brewer, still in his blue uniform, was the first to approach him with something other than a question. He had seen Guido, briefly, having a row with someone on the thirty-fourth floor on the morning of Hammond's murder.

Carl told his story over again to Chambrun, Johnny Thacker and I standing by.

"It may not be anything, Mr. Chambrun," Carl said.

"Anything about Guido is something, Carl," Chambrun said.

"I'd just taken over from Zorba the Greek," Carl said.

"Who?"

"Zacharapoulus, night elevator man," Johnny Thacker

explained. "Nobody can pronounce his name, so they call him—"

"Go on, Carl," Chambrun said.

"The panel was lit up with calls, all the way from the roof down. People coming down for breakfast, going to work. Regular morning rush of people going out. There was a passenger on my car, number four, waiting to go up. I didn't pay any attention to him because the Greek and I were making some wisecracks to each other. This passenger, standing behind me, said he wanted thirty-four when I started up. There were no up calls along the way and we zoomed right up to thirty-four. I opened the door and my passenger walked out—and right into Guido's breakfast wagon, which was coming around the corner from the service elevator." Carl grinned. "It was a first-class collision, like someone driving out of a side street right into a car on the main road. My passenger was off-balance and he staggered against the wall. He started to yell at Guido like a Marine sergeant. I tell you, I heard swear words like I never heard before, Mr. Chambrun. Normally I would have closed my door and gone on up to answer my calls, but I waited a moment because this guy, my passenger, sounded wild enough to make some kind of physical attack on Guido. Guido was shouting, too, but in Italian. He was trying to place things back in order on his wagon. That was all that concerned him. After my passenger had called him every kind of a Wop bastard you can think of, he turned away and went slowly down the hall. I gave Guido a thumbs-up, closed my door, and that was that. I guess it really isn't anything."

"Let me tell you how much it is, Carl," Chambrun said quietly. "Later, when Guido found the body in thirty-four-oh-six, he answered questions from the police and then he was sent home. He was pretty badly shaken up. But he told his wife there was something important he hadn't told me—about bumping into a man in the hall on thirty-four. He thought that man might have been

171

Geoffrey Hammond's breakfast guest."

"Oh, wow!" Carl said.

"Guido could have described him," Chambrun said. "How about you, Carl?"

The elevator man stared at Chambrun for a moment, searching, I thought, for a description. "I don't know if you know how it is, Mr. Chambrun. I carry hundreds and hundreds of people every morning. Most of them I notice getting in the car. They have to pass me, they look at me. A lot of them are familiar and I smile and say good-morning. But this fellow—well, he was already in the car when I took over from the Greek. The Greek and I, like I said, were joking. I just didn't look at the passenger. I was making some crack at the Greek as I closed the car door and started up. First run of the morning. I heard this guy behind me say, 'Thirty-four, please.' I didn't look around at him. I was thinking about some wisecrack I'd neglected to throw at the Greek."

"But he got off at thirty-four, and you held there to watch the row when he collided with Guido?"

"Yeah, but his back was to me, mostly. Guido was facing me."

"Some kind of description, man!" Chambrun said, sharp now. "Old? Young? Dark? Light? Tall? Short?"

"Medium height," Carl said, struggling to remember. "He had on a hat so I didn't see the color of his hair. Not young, I'd say. I'm sorry, Mr. Chambrun, I wouldn't know him if you brought him into this office."

Chambrun leaned back in his chair with a sigh. He was thinking, I guessed, that this man had a genius for being seen and yet not seen. Guido had been face to face with him, but Guido was dead before he could tell about it. Three others who had seen him were dead.

Carl started for the door, unhappy about his inability to give Chambrun what he wanted. At the door he stopped and turned back.

"There's one thing I forgot to mention," he said.

"Yes, Carl?" Chambrun asked.

"This guy was clumsy. He almost fell against the wall when Guido came whizzing around the corner with his wagon. Later, when he walked away down the hall I saw he was lame."

Chambrun was on his feet. "He was *what?*"

"Lame. A real gimpy leg. Could have been a phony. You've seen war veterans—you know what I mean?"

Chambrun looked at me, his eyes very bright. "That just could be your second head, Mark," he said.

CHAPTER FIVE

The case was over as far as I was concerned. Roy Conklin was clumsy and he had an artificial leg. He had the kind of ugly temper that matched the man who'd shouted curses at Guido.

There were things that didn't fit, but they were all things we'd accepted as fact from Conklin himself. He had told us he'd never been to High Crest in his life. He had told us that, when Hal Carpenter was murdered at the ski resort, he, Conklin, was in New York "minding the store." So those statements had to be proved lies. He had told us he had no idea who had breakfasted with Hammond. Another lie, of course. He was the breakfast guest and the killer. Carl Brewer would be a witness of sorts to place Conklin there.

So what was Joanna Fraser doing making martinis for him? Chambrun had a suggestion. "It was Miss Coyle who told us what Joanna saw that night," he said to Hardy, who had come to the office on the run to hear Carl Brewer's story. "She saw a man at the window of Carpenter's cabin. She watched him for a while and then 'he walked around

173

to the front door of the cabin.' Wasn't that it? She didn't say 'limped around to the front door.' Perhaps because she thought he was awkward in fairly deep snow, she didn't think of it as a disability. Didn't think of it as a means of identifying him.''

"So?" Hardy said.

"Hammond is murdered, the hotel is agog with it," Chambrun said. "Joanna is circulating in the lobby. She sees a man—and Conklin was here, God knows—sees him from behind, let's say, to make our case. Lame, limping! Something about the way he moved brought it all back to her. The picture-wire killer had just struck again, and here was a limping man, like the man outside Carpenter's cabin.''

"So she doesn't bother to tell anyone?" Hardy asked. "You're reaching, Pierre."

"A very straightforward, self-motivated lady," Chambrun said. "She wasn't sure. 'Play the game like a sportsman,' Dobler said. She walks boldly up to Conklin and says something like, 'Don't I know you from somewhere? Didn't we meet at High Crest in Colorado?' Conklin is stunned. He tells her she's mistaken. Joanna, still uncertain, goes up to her apartment to decide what to do. Has she really got something?

"Conklin knows he's up the creek. He can't leave the hotel. He can't run away. Somehow Joanna has to be dealt with before she talks to the cops. Conklin knows about her original testimony at High Crest. She saw a man at the window of Carpenter's cabin.''

"How does he know that?" Hardy asked.

"From Ziegler, the detective who was working for him at High Crest at the time. No time to waste for brother Conklin. He follows Joanna up to her apartment, sixteen eleven. He rings her bell. Joanna is making herself a drink. She goes to the door. Conklin is all apologies. How could he have been so stupid as not to remember? Of course they met at High Crest—at the time of Carpenter's murder. She must forgive him for drawing a blank, but his own close friend and business associate has just been killed in the same ghastly fashion. He had just drawn a blank when she spoke to him.

"Joanna is a friendly, outgoing person. She must have been wrong. He was Hammond's friend, a victim once removed, you might say. She was just making herself a drink, wouldn't he like to join her? He could, I'll bet he said, use a drink. And so they drink, chatting about murder, if you like. Something as simple as the need for an ashtray lets him move around behind her, and that is the end of Joanna Fraser."

"Takes time to wipe his fingerprints off glasses and whatever, and goes," Hardy said.

"If this isn't how it was, I'll buy you a steak dinner, Walter," Chambrun said. "And I've got another one to throw at you, perhaps more provable. Ziegler, the detective, had his office in Los Angeles. Conklin, who handles other personalities besides Hammond, undoubtedly had clients in the movie capitol. That was where Sharon Dain operated. Ziegler's client, I say Conklin, could have met her there. He hires Ziegler to find out what she was up to at High Crest. Conklin must have been in L.A., not here 'minding the store.' Money delivered to Ziegler by messenger in cash, wasn't it? If Conklin was in L.A. on legitimate business you should be able to find someone who knows it. Bobby Bryan could probably tell you who Conklin's clients were out there."

You may ask why we sat there theorizing instead of acting; why Conklin wasn't immediately placed under arrest. It was because Lieutenant Hardy was a very thorough man. He wanted to plug the holes in his case with something more tangible than Chambrun's guess work. Conklin wasn't going anywhere. He had a cop at his elbow. I know Hardy gave orders for that cop to be told that Conklin was now our prime suspect. Conklin's bank account might show that he had financed Sharon Dain's

175

defense. Sharon Dain, questioned in jail, would recall Conklin as a customer. No one had ever asked her that. If we placed him in Hollywood, we just about had him cold. The wheels were turning, but slowly. Fatally slowly, it turned out.

Bobby Bryan wasn't in his room. He and his bodyguard must be in the hotel or the bodyguard would have managed to get word to Hardy that they were taking off somewhere. I set out to find him to ask about Conklin's clients in L.A.

I found him. He was in the Trapeze Bar again, and Roy Conklin was with him again at the same corner table. I can't tell you what it was like to see Conklin sitting there, calmly drinking a Scotch on the rocks. The Conklin I now knew to be a killer! I couldn't ask Bobby my question in front of him.

"You two decided to live here?" I asked.

"It's all right, isn't it, as long as we pay the tab?" Conklin growled at me.

"Anything new?" Bobby asked.

I think now I must have been as transparent as a windowpane. I couldn't take my eyes off Conklin and he must have read what I was trying so hard to hide from him. I muttered something inane about looking for someone who might have seen someone who might have been recognized by Guido, the dead waiter, as Hammond's breakfast guest.

Conklin gave a sour little laugh. "Your Mr. Chambrun never lets go of an idea once he's proclaimed it, does he? For God sake, why would Geoffrey invite an enemy to breakfast? Count on it, the killer came in after the breakfast guest was gone, posing as a waiter for the wagon, or a maintenance man, or even a maid. Geoff was preoccupied with business, paid no attention to whoever it was."

"It could be, I suppose," I said.

"Hell, don't you even back up your resident mastermind?" Conklin pushed himself up. "I think I could use the plumbing," he said. I watched him limp away, pausing at the bar where the two cops, acting as bodyguards for these two guys, were sitting. A bodyguard for a killer! That was a new twist. I saw Conklin's man get off his stool and follow the lame man to the men's room at the far end of the bar.

I unloaded the word to Bobby Bryan then. He looked as if he thought I'd blown my stack as I started talking.

"Roy? You all have to be dreaming!"

"We need your help," I told him. "The names of any clients Conklin has in Hollywood; did he go there often; could he have been there at the time Hal Carpenter was murdered?"

We were both watching the door to the men's room. "I can give you half a dozen names in Hollywood," Bobby said. "Yes, Roy went out there three or four times a year, no special times. And remember, Roy told you himself that Geoffrey Hammond and I were in Switzerland at the time of the High Crest killing. I don't know where Roy was. He said he was in New York."

"We think not. We'd like to prove not."

Bobby took a pen and a notebook out of his pocket. He tore a page out of the book and began to write a list of names on it. I watched the men's room. Presently a couple of guys who had been at the bar went in together. Bobby handed me his slip of paper.

"Five names I can think of off the top of my head," he said.

One of the guys who had just gone into the men's room came running out shouting something at Eddie, the bartender. I couldn't hear what it was over the general noise of conversation. Eddie ducked out from behind the bar and ran into the men's. Instinctively, I knew we had trouble.

"Come on," I said to Bobby. We took his bodyguard along with us.

177

In the white-tiled men's room Eddie was bending over a man who was crumpled on the floor in one of the closed-in cubicles. Almost before I looked I knew it was going to be Conklin's guard.

"You see someone else with him?" I asked the two excited guys who had found the man.

Eddie looked up and saw me. "Better get Doc Partridge, Mark," he said. "This guy has had his skull smashed in."

I wasn't interested in the house physician just then. I was looking at the red fire door in the far wall of the men's room. Conklin was on the loose.

Conklin, you'd think, would not be a hard man to spot with that painful limp. That fire door opened out into the second-floor corridor, midway between my apartment and Chambrun's office and directly opposite the door to the main fire stairs, which ran from the penthouse on the roof to the subbasement—forty-one floors plus the two basement levels. All Conklin had to do was cross the hall and he could come out anyplace he chose in the hotel.

I ran into Chambrun's office to tell him and Hardy what had happened. Hardy set about alerting all his people, all the special guards. The people on our switchboard got through to all the staff people at their posts and they, in turn, contacted everyone who was on the move, like bellboys, elevator men, waiters, kitchen help. In ten minutes several hundred people were looking for one lame man on the run.

"He could have made it to one of the basement levels and out onto the street," was my contribution.

"He might not have been stopped," Chambrun said, "but he'd have been seen."

At the end of a half an hour, preliminary reports began to come in over Chambrun's phone. No one had seen a limping man anywhere. Then another call came and I saw Chambrun freeze in his chair. He reached forward and

178

turned on the squawk box so we could all hear the conversation.

"Chambrun? Is that you?"

It was Conklin. We all knew that harsh voice. Miss Ruysdale, always efficient, turned on the tape recorder.

"Where are you calling from, Conklin?"

"No reason not to tell you," Conklin said. "Your switchboard will tell you, if you check, that I'm in Mark Haskell's apartment."

"There's a cop there!" I said.

"There was a cop," Chambrun said. "Am I right, Conklin? There *was* a cop?"

Conklin laughed that sardonic laugh of his. "Your brilliance always amazes me, Chambrun. But I've called to make a deal."

"Naturally," Chambrun said. "You have Miss Coyle."

Hardy was gesturing frantically to one of his men, but Chambrun made a sharp countergesture.

"Tell your lieutenant to hold his water," Conklin said, almost as if he'd seen. "As you say, I have Miss Coyle. Lovely girl. Would not be so lovely if her face was contorted from strangling."

"Sonofabitch," I said in a voice I didn't recognize.

"Talk," Chambrun said.

"There must be a way out of here through one of the basements and to the street," Conklin said. "Fix it for me."

"No way," Chambrun said. "Everybody is alerted, looking for you."

"Come, come, Big Daddy. You can take me out and nobody would even look. I will, of course, have Miss Coyle with me. Arrange for a car to be left at the exit you choose. No driver. You will drive. When I get to where I want to go, you and Miss Coyle can have a drink together. If you screw it up, neither one of you will ever have another drink with anyone. How long will it take you to set things up?"

179

"Twenty minutes—half an hour to get a car here from the hotel garage."

"Fine," Conklin said. "I can read Hardy's mind, you know. Sharpshooters, tailing police cars. One twist of the wire and Miss Coyle has had it. When you're ready for me, just ring this phone." That was all.

Chambrun leaned back. "Call the garage, Ruysdale, and have a car delivered to the cellar exit on the north side."

Ruysdale flew to her own office.

"We can take him in five minutes, you know," Hardy said.

"If you want to pay the price," Chambrun said. "He has nothing to lose and everything to gain."

"And you're going to help him get away?" Hardy said.

Chambrun's cold eyes looked steadily at his friend. "Over my dead body, quite literally," he said.

I was sent to the subbasement to warn people to stay out of sight. The lame man, his hostage, and the boss were to be allowed to pass without question.

The journey to the basement kept me from knowing what Chambrun had planned, and I never did know till it was all over. When I got back to the office I was just in time to hear that the car had been delivered from the garage and to see Chambrun pick up his phone and tell Conklin that he was on his way.

What now seems like a long time later I got it all from Nora. When she told me, I was holding her in what I hoped she would know were strong, irresistible, masculine arms.

She had been in my apartment, reading. Her bodyguard-cop was sitting in his usual place by the door. There was a knock. The guard asked who it was.

"Relief man," a voice said.

The cop opened the door, and was hit over the head by Conklin, who had some kind of iron bar in his hand. We found out later it was the handle to a mop wringer kept in the Trapeze men's room. Conklin used it on both cops. Nora screamed, but he'd slammed the door shut. My place is soundproof, like most apartments in the Beaumont. He told her what her options were. Play it his way or she had none. He took a coil of picture wire from his pocket to emphasize the point. Then he called Chambrun.

And so eventually the time came when Chambrun called to say he was ready. At which point Conklin produced a gun and stood behind Nora. Ironically, Hardy had allowed Conklin to have that gun—to protect himself! He'd left the door on the latch. Chambrun knocked and let himself in.

"I was relieved," Nora told me, "but he looked like a stone statue. There was nothing about him that suggested any hope. That man!"

Conklin ordered Chambrun to empty his pockets, take off his coat. He wanted to be sure Chambrun wasn't armed. Satisfied, after slapping Chambrun all over, Conklin smiled and said, "It's your game, master. We follow the leader."

Down the deserted hallway they went, Chambrun leading the way, to the service elevator at the rear. The elevator was there, door propped open. Chambrun had made certain that there would be no delays during which some innocent bypasser might disrupt the whole procedure. You don't come on a girl in the hands of a strangler, with a wire around her neck and a gun at her back, without running screaming for help. Jerry Dodd and Hardy had tried to minimize that possibility. No elevators except the service car to stop at two; stairway and fire stairs blocked; the hallway on two shut off at each end.

Chambrun removed the block that propped open the door of the service car. Conklin and his hostage had moved in behind him.

"We are going down to the subbasement," he said, not turning his head. "We will then walk through the corridors there to the north side of the building where the car is waiting."

"Your ball game," Conklin said. "Just bear in mind that if you screw it up, I won't wait for explanations—or for one of your theories!"

Nora told me that as the service car started down, noiselessly, she felt as if her blood had turned to ice water, her legs were scarcely able to hold her up.

"I started to sag, Mark," she told me, "and that terrible wire began to tighten around my neck. My God, I had seen Joanna, you know."

The service car reached the subbasement.

"There's a long corridor with rooms opening off it," Nora said. "But you know that, Mark. I saw machinery of different sorts, and what looked like a laundry. But no people! It was almost like a tomb, lighted by bare electric bulbs spaced every few feet along the corridor. Chambrun walked ahead of me, never looking back. Conklin had his wire around my neck, held in one hand, and his gun, pointed at Chambrun's back, held in the other. And then—oh my God, Mark—all the lights went out and we were in total darkness."

Conklin shouted at Chambrun, demanding to know what had happened. No answer. Nora felt the wire starting to tighten around her neck.

"I'm warning you, Chambrun!" Conklin shouted.

"And then," Nora told me, "I heard Chambrun's voice. He was *behind* us now! 'What you feel pressed against your head, Conklin, is a gun,' he said, in the coldest voice I've ever heard. 'If you haven't dropped your gun and let go that wire in two heartbeats, they'll be scraping your brains off the side walls here.' "

" 'You haven't got a gun!' Conklin said."

" 'Try me,' Chambrun said. 'I start counting now—up to two!' I felt the wire loosen, Mark, and I guess I dropped down on my knees—on all fours as a matter of fact. I think I heard Conklin's gun drop on the stone floor. And suddenly all the lights were on again and the corridor was crowded with people who swarmed over Conklin. Chambrun was there, and he *did* have a gun. He handed it to a big man with a grey walrus mustache and said 'Thanks, Mac. Handled perfectly.' Then he came over to me and helped me, gently, to stand up. 'You're a gutsy girl, Miss Coyle,' he said. 'But it's all over now, quite finally over.' "

It was a day or so before we had the pieces all put together, because Conklin never spoke a word, never offered any explanation.

Of course what had happened in the subbasement was obvious enough, even before Chambrun explained it. The man with the grey walrus mustache was McPherson, our daytime engineer. He had been stationed in one of the side rooms off the corridor with a gun and a clear way to signal a man on the master control board. As Chambrun reached that doorway McPherson signaled and the lights went out. Chambrun took a quick step to the right in the darkness and he was suddenly armed. End of Conklin as a threat.

And the Conklin story? It was put together with the help of Sharon Dain, released from custody in Colorado, by Bobby Bryan, and by Chambrun's theories, which had to be fact.

It had started, a long way back, with a handsome, arrogant man named Conklin being shot down by Israeli commandos in an Arab town. The loss of his right leg crippled Conklin in more ways than one, psychologically as well as physically. Always successful with women, Conklin now felt mutilated, ugly, ashamed. He saw himself forever shut off from romantic seductions. He turned to the business of buying his sex from women who didn't care whether he had one leg or three, as long as he paid the price. On a trip to Los Angeles some two and a half years ago he had encountered Sharon Dain, a hard-boiled hooker. What there was about Sharon that overwhelmed him, I don't know, but Conklin fell in love with her. She laughed at him when he suggested marriage. But she played along with him on succeeding visits because he might, with his connections, get her the only thing she wanted, a career in films.

That January, two years ago—with Hammond and Bobby Bryan in Switzerland—he took off for L.A. to make another pitch to Sharon Dain. He couldn't find her. Questions produced the fact that she had gone to High Crest with a man. That was when he went into the elaborate routine of hiring Al Ziegler, the private eye, to go to High Crest to find out what was cooking. Ziegler reported that she was having her ears beaten off by a sadistic punk. And so Conklin drove to High Crest, slipped into the grounds at night and, looking through the window of Carpenter's cabin, saw his ladylove being pounded unconscious. He went in and killed her tormentor. Where the technique of the picture wire came from we never knew, but he was prepared to do it that way.

"An old terrorist technique," Chambrun said. "The silent murder in a dark alley. We used it during the days of the French Resistance in Paris."

So Conklin slipped away from High Crest, unaware that anyone had seen anything. Sharon would come back to her Hollywood haunts and he could approach her again. But that never happened because the police arrested her for the murder he'd committed.

"This haunted him," Chambrun told us in a final session on the case, two days after Conklin's arrest. "He got reports from Ziegler for a few more days so he knew the defence committee hadn't been able to raise enough money to hire Max Steiner to defend Sharon. It had to be found, and he knew where."

This part of it came from Bobby Bryan. Geoffrey Hammond kept a large sum of money in a special account. This was money acquired through Hammond's highly sophisticated blackmail techniques in the Middle East.

"Roy had access to that account, as Geoff's business manager," Bobby told us. "If Hammond was across the world somewhere and needed funds, Roy could produce them for him."

"So then, with Hammond in Switzerland with you," Chambrun said, "he produced two hundred thousand dollars for Sharon's defense."

"I doubt if he stole the whole amount from Hammond," Bobby said. "Roy had made a lot of dough himself from those Arab oil sheiks. I suspect what he put up at first was his own. But then Steiner's costs mounted and mounted, and he had to dig into Hammond's special account. The money was kept the way it was to avoid taxes. Roy took it, expecting to find a way to get it back before Hammond found out. But he didn't find a way."

"Which led to three more deaths," Chambrun said, "so long after the first one. I guess again, gentlemen. Hammond discovered his special account was short. Only Conklin had access, could account for it. He invited Conklin for breakfast. Conklin, who had never been able to repay the money, sensed disaster. He came prepared—you might say wired for murder."

"And so the snowball started rolling," Hardy said. "We'll never know for certain, but you must have been right about Joanna Fraser. An encounter in the lobby, he follows her upstairs, gets invited in, and he's still safe."

"Then Ziegler-Davis shows up and tries to get him to expose himself. Conklin was perfectly willing to kill a dozen people by now to stay hidden," Chambrun said.

"All for love of a cold-hearted hooker who didn't give a damn about him," Hardy said. The Lieutenant was happy. He had his case.

"Mark might not agree with the words 'cold-hearted,' Walter," Chambrun said. "She provided Conklin, a sick man, with some kind of warmth, some kind of simulated tenderness, for which he was grateful enough to kill for her." He put out his cigarette. "Well—" he began.

I raised my hands in a gesture of surrender. "I know, boss, I know," I said. "We still have a hotel to run."

A FEW CLUES ABOUT MORE GREAT TITLES YOU'LL SOON BE SEEING IN KEYHOLE CRIME

THE BLOOD ON MY SLEEVE
Ivon Baker

Matthew Kendrick steals, amongst other things, a Picasso, a Monet and an eighteenth-century vase from five wealthy men in the USA. It is simply his way of protesting against art investment and the cache is recovered intact shortly after. But Matthew Kendrick is found dead, so archaeologist David Meynell returns to England to find the killer of his former student — and whilst tracking down the murderer, narrowly escapes death himself.

RANSOM TOWN
Peter Alding

Detective Inspector Fusil of Fortrow CID had never heard of the Organisation for Social Equality when it demanded a payment of a million pounds — but he knew it was serious when a dutch barn went up in flames and was followed by a fire bomb explosion. As the arson became more intensive, could he work fast enough to save the countless lives which hung in the balance?

 Keyhole Crime

LETTER OF INTENT
Ursula Curtiss

The anonymous letter was capable of blowing her world to pieces: 'I've been waiting for this. If you don't call off the wedding, I will'.

Celia Brett had been a dowdy inarticulate girl of eighteen when she began working for the rich and pleasant Stevensons. But her apparent innocence concealed a ruthless social climber who had played her part in two shocking tragedies. And now a third lay lurking . . .

THE BURGLAR IN THE CLOSET
Lawrence Block

It was ridiculous really — there was Bernie Rhodenbarr, professional burglar, locked in the closet of a small New York apartment while thieving it. And there was his swag, all neatly packed, on the opposite side of the bedroom.

When Bernie finally got out he wasn't too pleased to find the jewels gone and Crystal Sheldrake, their beautiful owner, dead on the mat with a steel instrument in her heart. The cops weren't too pleased either . . .

Look out for them wherever you normally buy paperbacks

 Keyhole Crime

If you have any difficulty obtaining any of these titles, or if you would like further information on forthcoming titles in Keyhole Crime please write to:-

Keyhole Crime, PO Box 236, Thornton Road, Croydon, Surrey CR9 3RU.